Farewell to Peace

Kyuka Lilymjok

i

ISBN 9789789547548

Published by:
Free Pen Publishers
10 Lachlan Close, Maitama, Abuja

To the memories of all the martyrs of Justice

Peace is
nobody's birthright.
Justice is everyone's
birthright.

Chapter One

It was a dark cloudy morning. The sun like a millipede was climbing out of Sekia Mountains that surrounded Sekia forest like a city fence. A tall, wiry, middle-aged man with a young man were making their way through the treacherous rocky path of the forest towards the Sekia Mountains about seven kilometers away. The elderly man led the way followed by the youngster. The elderly man wore a military-style fez cap, a rugged safari jacket and military boots. But for the black color of his fez cap and safari jacket, he could pass for a military man. The youngster wore a beret, a dark tee-shirt, faded jeans and sneakers. He could easily pass for a hippie or rudeboy.

Though the weather was pleasant, there was little pleasantness on the face of the tall wiry man making his way through the ragged environment to the Sekia Mountains. His face was as scraggy and threadbare as the terrain he was trudging. It was as if the treacherous path he was hauling through was leaving its footprints on his face more than he was leaving any footprints on it. The fact however was that the condition of the man's face had nothing to do with the rigor of hauling through the broken path to the mountains. Neither was he born with such a coarse face. Rather, anger and bitterness deep inside him had migrated from his heart to eat up his face leaving pockmark troughs and highlands on it. Ancient in origin as the anger and bitterness that bore them, the pockmarks on the man's face had spiked with time such that an ant hauling through his face would not find it less rugged and treacherous than he was finding the path he was hauling through.

Though the path was winding and hilly, the elderly man was picking his way through the forest with unusual ease familiarity had bred. Not so however the young man following him. A marked unease could be discerned from the way he was tagging the elderly man. While the elderly man was born and grew up in the neighborhood of the mountainous region they were, the youngster was not. Not only was the elderly man a native of the neighborhood, he had at an early age familiarized himself with the forest they were hauling through and the mountains they were headed for. The young man on the other hand was not a native of the country they were and was going through the forest for the first time. Not only did he not know the forest, he only met the elderly man two days ago. He met him at a beer parlour the two men got talking. 'My name is Belaru; what's yours?' the elderly man had said to him with a lot of verve and charm.

'I am Dakas,' he had replied the elderly man.

'Yeah, 'Belaru whirred. 'So Dakas how is life? How are things generally?'

'Life is what it has always been – messy, and things are what they will always be – tough.'

'Yeah,' Belaru groaned. 'The despicable system; the iniquitous system; the abominable system,' he swore under his breath, then sank into a turbulent silence while the two men drank. Later, they talked a lot more and seemed to share the same views on life and how it could be made better.

They left the beer parlour late in the night with a promise to meet the following day at Belaru's place. They met the following day and talked a lot more ending in the beer parlour again. They left the beer parlour with an agreement to go to the Sekia Mountains the next day. It was Belaru that suggested the trip and Dakas perhaps under the influence of alcohol had agreed without giving the matter a thought.

Today the effect of alcohol had worn off, yet he found himself following Belaru to the Sekia Mountains without much intelligence of what they were going to the mountains for beyond the fact that the mountains were a great natural sight. Belaru had an uncanny pull on him that he could neither understand nor explain, but it was there. Walking behind Belaru on their way to the mountains, he heard the elderly man saying, 'I can never forget nor forgive those who killed my father.'

'Your father was killed?' Dakas asked.

'Yes, my father was killed by the despicable system; the iniquitous system; the abominable system,' Belaru said in a voice full of bitterness. 'Shortly after he was killed, my mother was also killed by the same people.'

'That was terrible,' said Dakas in a voice that conveyed empathy. 'Who were the people who did this to you?'

'Free trade,' Belaru said with a haunting anger.

'Free trade?' Dakas asked, puzzled.

'Yes, free trade.'

'I don't understand.'

"By free trade, developed nations pushed their products to us killing our industries that cannot produce goods of equal quality and sell at the same price with the incoming goods. My father worked in a textile industry. Quality and cheap fabrics from developed countries were imported into our country as required by free trade. These cheap fabrics killed the textile company my father was working as it killed other textile companies around the country. My father was laid off. Unable to take it, he had stroke and died. My mother unable to cope without him died a year later. That was how I became an orphan at the age of seven.

'That was tough,' Dakas said in a heavy tone.

'It was indeed tough,' Belaru said. 'You now see why I said free trade killed my parents?'

'Yes, I can now see,' Dakas said.

'But not to worry, they will hear from me at the right time; that's, if they are not already hearing from me,' Belaru said, somberly.

'Who are they that would hear from you and what will they hear from you?' Dakas asked.

'The system – developed nations and international economic institutions that insist on free trade,' Belaru said. 'I will hit back and hit back badly.'

Chapter Two

At the time Belaru was born, Bongoder was the king of Gebas. In the whole of his life, Bongoder had never understood why he should work for his sustenance, lest his prosperity. He had always schemed to get his sustenance and prosperity from the labour or wealth of others. Anyone who knew his father knew why he was what he was. His father throughout his life was a man it could be justifiably said never turned up an honest penny. He lived on others by tricks, subterfuge and treachery. He hated labour as if it were leprosy; as if it were something the cat brought in. He hated labour like sin.

How his father got the money to buy two oxen to be doing most of his laborious work Bongoder did not know and didn't think anyone beside his father knew. However he got it, Bongoder could swear it was neither by labour nor honest means. He must have employed some tricks, subterfuge or treachery to get it. At a time everyone in his district was using his hands to farm, his father was using oxen to farm. Poorly fed and poorly treated, his father worked his oxen in the farm from morning till night without much time for rest.

The oxen could farm, but could not weed. Bongoder's father tricked local women to weed for him on the promise that after harvest, he would pay them for their labour with the crops they weeded for him – promises he never got round to redeeming. He always found reasons not to give the women what he agreed to give either because harvest was bad or he had suffered a misfortune that made it impossible for him to perform his own side of the bargain. He was a promissory note no one really got round to cashing. He was seen by everyone as a man one will never enter into any business transaction with and not be cheated by him. That was why he kept losing labourers and employing new ones. Surprisingly he never lacked labourers though he was largely known as a shyster and a crook. There were always new people willing to be preyed on by him. Though they never got much from him, they kept coming to be exploited. It seemed people liked to be promised something though they knew or at least suspected nothing would be made from what was promised than being promised nothing at all. The preponderance of poverty in Bongoder's district and human nature that thrives on hope played so well into his father's hands.

In the dry season, the oxen carry Bongoder's father's crops from the farm to the house and from the house to the market. He even had more people outside the farm working for him than he had on the farm. The reason was that while virtually everyone had something to do in his own farm, many people once farm work was done, had little to do at home and so were likely to be working for his father.

One day Bongoder was sitting outside the house when he heard his father also sitting outside under a shade saying to a friend that there was nothing as gratifying as sitting under a shade while others are working for you under the sun.

'That's true,' the friend who was a lower version of his father said. 'It is like someone holding the cow and receiving all the kicks while you milk the cow.'

'I sometimes wonder why I still find labourers though I pay so little for what people do for me,' his father said. 'I still wonder why many people want to lend me labour when I had not paid for the one I earlier borrowed.'

'I think for many people it is better to lend labour in the vain hope of being paid for it than not lending it and watching it waste away,' his father's friend said. 'You cannot easily turn labour into money the way you can turn money into goods. Neither can you hoard it the way you can hoard money. You hoard labour and you die with it. You hoard money and you die leaving it for your family.'

'I see what you are saying,' his father said laughing. 'Because labour is a perishable commodity, it has to be used or it perishes. Therein lies my luck.'

'Your luck and mine further lies in the fact that there is so much poverty around; people need money and we are the ones that have little if not much of it. So, we dictate the terms of labour.'

'And how much we pay for commodities sold to us.'

'And that as well. The cheating system, the ratty system; the sneaky system.'

'Bongoder,' he heard his father calling him.

'Father,' he answered running to where his father and his friend were sitting.

'Go to my room and bring my smoking pipe and my walking stick.'

'Yes, father.'

His father smoked a lot and smoked only with a pipe. Long after stick cigarette came, his father went on using his pipe when other smokers had switched from pipe to stick cigarette. He rarely went anywhere without his smoking pipe. For many, it was what announced his presence wherever he went. And he had a sloppy way of holding it in his hand or mouth that always impressed Bongoder. Holding it by the tail, the pipe lopped or dangled about as if it would fall from his hand or mouth. Though lopping, the cigarette burning in the pipe rarely spilled on the ground. Like the pipe, his father rarely went anywhere without his walking stick though he did not need it. He was not stooping in his walk and therefore needed not the support of a walking stick. So he concluded he was using the stick more as a status symbol or out of habit.

Chapter Three

Bongoder was not from Gebas' royal family, but became king when his family dethroned the Tonwill royal family. At the time he was born and thereafter, Gebas had a very powerful monarchy. Bongoder's father finding himself with means began plotting how he would ascend the royal throne after the then king. In his reckoning, this would guarantee his chances of feeding on others the way the Tonwill family had been. When he started nursing the ambition of becoming king, he began warming his way into the hearts of palace politicians in the king's court. Using bribes, soon he was sitting as king in the hearts of some of the courtiers if not over Gebas. Here and there some of the courtiers began dropping his name randomly as someone who would make a good king.

But three things were against Bongoder's father becoming king and one of these things ultimately proved fatal to his ambition. First, he was not from the royal family that produced kings. Secondly, he had established a nasty reputation of being mean and feeding on others. Thirdly, the ruling king was young and was not likely to die before his father. Of these three factors that weighed against him, his father thought the third was the weightiest and proved so in the end. Being not from the royal family was not a very strong factor because the Tonwill royal family had not always been the royal family. It seized the throne from another family and this fact was known by everyone in Gebas because it was fairly recent. The Tonwill royal family were bandits that fell upon the kingdom, put the royal family to the sword and usurped the throne. Not many people wept for the royal family that was dethroned because it was seen by many as a family of rascals and bloodsuckers.

When the Tonwill family seized the reins of power, rumor started circulating that Tonwill the king was an armed robber and the son of a prostitute. In power, the royal family did not conduct itself with the dignity and nobility expected of royalty. Cases of the family capturing people and selling them into slavery though slavery had long been abolished abounded. Cases of it buying slaves from other countries to work for it also abounded. So also cases of the family seizing landed property of the people and even their farm produce also abounded. Like the previous royal family, this royal family looked like one not many people would weep for if it was kicked out of the throne.

Bongoder's father was a vermin and most people knew this. But so was the Tonwill family. In addition to being vermins, the Tonwill family was a family of bandits. Many people thought a vermin was better than a bandit particularly when Bongoder's father turned generous to the courtiers of the king's court. Some sophisticated people even started thinking and murmuring in the dark that man by nature is a vermin who seeks divine authority for his vermination by saying everything was created for him.

But the last factor against Bongoder's father becoming king held. The king he wanted to succeed was a young man who was most likely to survive him. At some point Bongoder's father thought of killing him, after all his family wiped out the former royal family to ascend the throne, but thought better of it.

Bongoder left home fairly early, but not too early to imbibe the values of his father. He left home not necessarily of his own accord, but his father's. His father wanted him to go into the world to feed on others the way he was feeding on Gebas so that together they could build an empire of vermination. When time started running against him, the father asked the son to return home so that he would transfer his ambition of becoming king to the son.

When Bongoder got home, his father started introducing him to courtiers of the king's court who anyway already knew him, if not physically, by reputation. As he was introducing the son, he was firming up in the son the three principles of vermination he had always strove to drum into him albeit in a subtle manner: Suck the blood of your victim because he would not give it to you were you to request. If you don't suck the blood of others, you will go anemic and die. No one becomes rich by his effort alone.

'Pettas,' this is Bongoder my son,' Bongoder's father said while introducing his son to one of the palace politicians in the king's court. 'I mean my son that has not been in the kingdom but has now returned home.'

'The one that is the chip of the old block?' Pettas said smiling slyly at Bongoder. 'Of course, I know him.'

The one that is the chip of the old block Bongoder repeated to himself what Pettas said. What did he mean by the chip of the old block? He was not the only son of his father. He was not even the first. His father had tried cajoling his first son to be a vermin like him, but he had refused. Failing to get him follow his footsteps, he turned to Bongoder and found in him a willing son. Was Pettas alluding to his character or his physical appearance? He looked very much like his father. But so did his other siblings. In the circumstance, he had no way of knowing which was which or what was what.

Matters went the way Bongoder's father wanted them to go and Bongoder became the king of Gebas after the one his father wanted to succeed died. This happened long after his father's death. Though it happened long after his death, Bongoder had forgotten nothing of the principles of vermination his father inculcated in him. He ascended the throne with these principles firmly enthroned in his mind. They were what he would apply in his governance of Gebas and exploitation of the world.

Chapter Four

As king, Bongoder increased local taxes. Before there was no tax on farmlands and farm produce. He imposed tax on these properties. As king, he was the owner of all lands and the crops produced from these lands. People could not be living off the fat of the land without paying for it. Living off the fat of the land without paying meant they would be growing fatter while he will be shrinking when the opposite ought to be the case.

'When these taxes were introduced, there was an outcry by farmers who would bear its brunt. 'Why should I pay taxes on the land I inherited from my father and on the crops grown on such land when my father did not pay such taxes?' one of the farmers wondered aloud to a fellow farmer.

'I am still panting from the shock of these taxes,' the other farmer said. 'How can a king place such heartless taxes on our plates and tongues? A king is supposed to place food on the plates and tongues of his subject; why is our king placing famine and hunger on our plates and tongues?'

'These taxes are mean and cynical.'

'They are indeed cruel.'

When Bongoder heard this exchange between the two farmers, he said to Pettas, 'how is a king to be fat without living off the fat of the people?' Of all his courtiers, Pettas appeared to him the most servile, devious and sycophantic. He seemed to have travelled when conscience was being shared. You could only trust him when your eyes were on him. The moment he turned the corner and you could no longer see him, your trust should stop at the corner. He was as sycophantic as any courtier can be. Cases of his sycophancy were embarrassing to any decent mind. He was eating food with the king one day when the king suddenly lost appetite. 'This food is not delicious,' the king said pushing away his plate.

'Since the king said the food is not delicious; it is also not delicious to me,' Pettas said also pushing away his plate.

One day, the king went for a meeting taking place upstairs. As he was climbing the staircase, he overheard Pettas saying whether a car should be brought to take the king up. The king stifled a laugh that possessed him.

One of the king's councilors had not been attending council meetings for a long while because he was taking care of his ailing father. When he eventually turned up at the council, though the king knew why he had not been in council, he upbraided him, rather too severely.

'The way you scolded him Your Majesty is the right way to deal with errants like him,' Pettas who knew the councilor's condition as anyone said.

Other councilors at the meeting looked askance and screwed their faces in disgust of what Pettas said.

Before becoming a courtier, Pettas was a member of a political group whose chairman told him he would not be seeking re-election into his office again.

'That's impossible,' Pettas said. 'Only you can be the chairman of our group.' Meanwhile he Pettas wanted to be the next chairman.

Despite Pettas's nasty reputation as a sycophant, surprisingly king after king took him seriously so much that he was the closest confidant and ally of many kings including Bongoder. It seemed there was a pathetic craving by kings for their asses to be licked, and Pettas was there to lick their asses. Later, Bongoder understood that the conditions of kings including himself were worse than he earlier thought. Most kings were averse to truth. Sycophants merely exploited this condition of kings. Exploiting this condition, kings were reduced to mere puppets in the hands of sycophants.

'I wonder,' Pettas said on this occasion that Bongoder was chiding farmers lamenting his new taxes. He was not only looking amused, he was looking like one personally offended by the remarks of the farmers.

'Taxes are what you pay for being alive,' Bongoder said. 'Being alive, they must pay taxes.'

'That's true.'

'Haven't they heard the saying that there are only two things one can be sure of: death and taxes.'

Pettas laughed heartily.

'Elsewhere I learned there were taxes that were paid even by the dead.'

'You don't mean it your majesty,' Pettas said. For the first time since Bongoder knew him, something like disbelief of what the king said appeared on his face and something that looked like the tail of conscience appeared with this thing. This more than anything told the king what he said sounded not only very bizarre to Pettas, but untenable. Even his sycophantic flim* that suppressed and tamed his involuntary reaction to express truth failed to suppress or tame this one.

The second thing Bongoder did on becoming king was to advise his subjects who were crafty or were rich and strong to go to other lands to establish

---

* Sycophantic flim in Coocuk mythology was a gland in the heard of a sycophant that secretes juices that prevent a sycophant from expressing the truth.

dominion over these lands and be repatriating back home proceeds of their exploitation of these lands.

Inkan and Pouker were some of the countries Bongoder asked some of his subjects to go to suck their juices and pass them to Gebas. Quite a number of his subjects heeded his call seeing in it robust possibilities of enriching themselves by the wealth of others and extending the influence of Gebas around the world.

Chapter Five

Slando sent to Inkan by Bongoder took over their land to produce cotton needed by textile industries all over the world to produce clothes. When Slando got to Inkan he found most of the land of the kingdom lying fallow. Most of the indigenous people were hunters, fruit gatherers while a few were into subsistence farming.

It was a popular saying of Slando that day and night he threw his mind about as if it was a net the fisherman throws about at sea. Throwing his mind about, whenever it falls where something good would sprout; where a big fish was, it would be flitting about the spot like a butterfly or in his words, dancing about the spot to the flute and drum of the place until the thing that would sprout, sprout or the fish that was about entered the net.

Slando had no money before he went to Inkan and had none when he got there. When he got to the country, he started throwing his mind around for how to come by means in a country he knew no one but wanted things to start happening for him quick. There were huge agricultural resources in Inkan and these resources were not exploited. Seeing this opportunity, he decided to settle for farming. But he needed money to spring out of the woods of agriculture. Throwing his mind about for a day or so, tricks of how to make it big in this kingdom sprouted in his fecund mind. He would make friends with Barbar and marry his daughter.

Barbar was a trusting and carefree man of moderate means. He was the first person Slando struck up friendship with in Inkan. He had a daughter he had been wanting to marry out, but had not found a good suitor for. When Slando started throwing his mind around for how to start up something in Inkan, his mind fell on Barbar and his daughter. For a while, his mind flitted about Barbar and his daughter dancing to the flute they were playing and the drum they were beating until a trick came up. He would marry Barbar's daughter. This would provide him the means he was looking for to start something big in Inkan.

Slando started deploying his charm towards Barbar's daughter the moment he made up his mind; and he had so much charm. In no time he was married to Barbar's daughter.

Barbar was a subsistence farmer who left things lying around for others to pick. He had a lot of farmlands he inherited from his father much of which he was not farming. When Slando asked him to give him some of his farmland for cultivation,

Barbar gave him the much of his farmlands that he wanted. Labour was cheap in Inkan. When Slando got land from Barbar, his father-in-law also gave him some money to cultivate these lands.

'Barbar, are you sure you are doing the right thing?' Tedis, Barbar cousin asked Barbar. 'You barely know this man and you have not only married off your daughter to him, you are giving him so much land and money to cultivate it.'

'True, I don't know him much; but I think I can trust him,' Barbar said.

'I don't trust him. He looks like a sneaking rat to me,'Tedis said. 'With his shifty eyes, he inspires no trust in me.'

'Let's give him the benefit of doubt.'

'The tick knows where to fasten itself to suck the cow or the sheep,' Tedis said. 'It fastens itself on an artery of the cow or sheep where it will be nibling away the viaticum of the cow or sheep.'

'The swine,' Slando swore at Tedis when he heard what the latter was saying about him. 'The swelling swine! As if the land and money are his.'

The first year Slando began farming in Inkan was a good farming year. Slando harvested a lot of crops from the farmlands Barbar gave him. In the space of ten years, Slando who came to Inkan without two nickels to rub together was a very rich man with farmlands all over the country.

'This is what happens when one throws his mind in the right direction and listens to the flutes and drums of places something good can sprout,' Slando said to himself. 'A few years ago, I was as broke as a tooth fairy; as broke as a joke. Today I am as rich as Croesus. Lyrics from the flute are intoxicating now. The drumbeats have risen to their crescendo and my dancing steps are quickening. I am in the dance of my life.'

Barbar, Slando's father- in-law died a couple of years after Slando began striking it rich in Inka. Shortly after his death, his daughter married to Slando also died. With the death of Barbar and his daughter, all Barbar farmlands became those of Slando.

When Bongoder learned of Slando exploits in Inkan, he encouraged him to take more Gebas people to Inkan to take over the land of this nation as Slando had done. Most of these newcomers to Inkan made it by means not too different from those Slando made it.

Chapter Six

Bongoder sometimes shrank with fear from the possible consequences of the vermination activities of Gebas around the world. Bedbugs, ticks, rats and even lice now and then get expelled by some drastic action of the host they are parasiting on. Fed up to his back teeth, the host sometimes pour acids and other chemicals on vermins that had been feeding on him so perniciously. Often, Bongoder fear this would be the fate of Gebas if its hosts around the world wake up to its vermination.

Gebas' vermination activities which began in the crude and vulgar form of slavery and colonialism, later became so subtle and refined that even the host sometimes was oblivious of the fact that he was the victim of vermination. Trade, loans, investment were the tools of Bongoder's subtle and refined vermination. Exploitation of the labours of others through slavery and colonialism amassed so much wealth for him and Gebas in products and money that Bongoder started wondering what he would do with this wealth. Soon it occurred to him he could process the produce in the farms and barns of his country to sell to other countries else they waste away. But he could not use his hands to process these produces. He needed machines to do it. He got some of his subjects to fabricate machines to process these produces for sale to other nations. Soon Gebas had machines processing produce of slave labour to products it was selling to other nations for prices fixed by Gebas. Gebas was able to fix prices for the processed products it sold to other countries because there were no such products in the nations it sold the products. Gebas' products were so attractive to these nations that they thought Gebas was doing them a favour selling the products to them despite their exorbitant prices. Though Gebas was verminating them, they were insensible to the vermination. Through trade, Gebas was making money it could not make through slavery and colonialism, yet there was no anger or protests from the hosts Gebas was sucking. Bongoder quickly understood what was happening. Though sucking of a host by a vermin takes more blood from the host to the vermin, it was the stinging edge of a bite that makes the host to immediately swing his arm to swat the vermin. Sucking has a dull edge that does not immediately wakes the host to his condition until he is almost going anemic. Slavery and colonialism were when Gebas as a vermin was biting the host and getting swatted by the host for doing so. The stinging bites of slavery and colonialism were so sharp that arms were swinging at Gebas on land and at sea. Slaves rebelled against Gebas on land and at sea; in the farms and at home. Slaves rebellion claimed the lives of many of Gebas' subjects on land and at sea. For instance, slaves uprising in a slave ship on the Atlantic Ocean was what led to slaves taking over Naisal Island and turning it into a nation. The slave uprising in the ship claimed all Gebas' subjects on board the ship.

The slaves in a long festering conspiracy the slave owners on board the ship did not detect unchained themselves and abruptly attacked their owners, collected the keys to their chains and unchained themselves. After unchaining themselves, they made sure they killed all Gebasites on board before fleeing the ship and swimming to Naisal island not far off.

Colonized people railed against Gebas clamouring for freedom; mouthing oppression and injustice. Now and then, noise about injustice and oppression in the colonies diminished to a distant echo only to come back in louder tones. For how much? Bongoder thought. For trifles. Worse, Gebas had the burden of administering the colonists. For all its pains, it saw no gratitude. Around the world, Gebas was fighting costly wars to suppress resentment to colonial rule that was not raking in much. For a long time Gebas kept wondering why it was taking so much bashing for little profit; so much pain for little gain. It ended colonialism and promoted free trade.

With free trade, Gebas sucks more blood and has no burden of administering any place it is taking its goods to. For all its pickings and takings, all Bongoder could see was pleasure and satisfaction on the faces of Gebas' victims. Not many were even grumbling against Gebas or him until the Tendu-Purgers came with their mission of purging vermination around the world.

Chapter Seven

Gebas' trading in goods led it to trading in services. It was Shoreline Oil Corporation in Gebas Bongoder sent to Bimigan to trade in services in that country. There was oil in Bimigan, but no one knew. Bongoder had the rare fortune of knowing there was oil in this nation and the additional fortune of having an oil corporation that could exploit it.

Shoreline Oil Corporation though an oil corporation did not go to Bimigan with much capital to harness the oil resources of this country. However, the corporation went to the country with a basket of tricks of how to make it in a foreign land without money. As soon as it got to Bimigan, its officials started ingratiating themselves with authorities of Bimigan. There was oil in the country. The Corporation would partner with the government to harness it if the government would invest by buying machineries that would be used to prospect for the oil and produce it. Whichever oil was produced its value would be shared fifty-fifty after deduction of operational cost. Shoreline corporation was entitled under the deal to repatriate home all its share under the deal after earning it. This agreement with Bimigan government was to last ninety years before it was reviewed.

Bimigan government desperate for its oil resources to be exploited, acceded to the agreement and began heavy investment into the process of exploiting the oil resources of the country. Under the agreement, Shoreline Oil Corporation was the operator on account of its technical knowhow while Bimigan government was the financier on account of its having money to invest in the enterprise.

As operator, it was Shoreline corporation that knew the equipment needed for exploration and production of oil. So, the money for purchasing this equipment was given to the corporation by Bimigan government. The government had no idea about the quality of these equipment nor their prices. It relied on the corporation for intelligence on price and the quality of the equipment. Here the corporation was laughing to the bank while the government was crying home.

'A corporation can't be in a sweeter position than this,' the Managing Director of Shoreline corporation said to the field operations manager. 'It is like being given a blank cheque on which you can enter any amount.'

'It is like lending money to the owner of the money and expecting him to pay heavy interest on his money,' the field operations manager said.

'This much that we are raking in from purchase of equipment is nothing near what we will be raking in from operational cost which is another open cheque,' the Managing Director said.

'Operational cost is indeed our main area of profit in this deal,' the field operations manager said. 'Operations are so complex with many twists and turns that we can be hiding in some nooks or crannies of these twists and turns to nibble off a lot for ourselves.'

'We can easily do what you are saying considering that our partner is not involved in the operational journey,' the Managing Director said. 'We can't have a better deal.'

'In one trip, we shall be collecting transport fares from the same passengers in three different stations,' the field operations manager said. 'We are paid at the station of purchasing equipment, at the station of operations, and at the station of sharing the value of oil produced.'

'What you are saying is that we have upstream, midstream and downstream payments,' the Managing Director said, laughing.

'That's it,' the field operations manager said, also laughing. 'And this will go on for ninety years. Just imagine how much blood we are going to suck for Gebas all these years. Just imagine how worse off these illiterate and ignorant country would be in the course of these years of our verminating it.'

The joint-venture agreement between Shoreline oil corporation and Bimigan government went into implementation the moment it was signed by both parties. Within ten years of Shoreline exploration and exploitation of oil in Bimigan, the corporation emerged one of the leading oil corporations in the world with capital assets spanning the world. As the corporation rose in financial power, Gebas rose in economic and political power. Gebas government ensured the corporation paid taxes to it and also ensured it remitted home a certain percentage of its earnings in Bimigan and other countries around the world for investment in critical economic sectors in Gebas.

While Gebas was prospering from oil exploitation in Bimigan by Shoreline oil corporation, Bimigan the country with the oil had little prosperity to show for its oil. But if Bimigan had no prosperity to show for its oil, it had environmental pollution and degradation to show. The coastal region of the country was so severely polluted and degraded that neither fishing nor farming could be done in the region which before oil exploitation produced food and fishes for local consumption and export.

Chapter Eight

Trading in foreign nations either in goods or services, opened Gebas' eyes to opportunities of lending money to these kingdoms and investing in them. Lending money to other kingdoms and investment in them later turned out more lucrative than even trade.

Trade in goods produced in Gebas led to other nations wanting to produce what Gebas was producing. Producing what Gebas was producing required funds which these nations did not have. So Gebas moved in to lend them the money they did not have but needed to produce what Gebas was selling to them.

Lending money to foreign nations turned out a very profitable venture. High interest on lending made it a very good business. So high was the interest on Gebas' loans to foreign nations that it never wanted its debtors to repay their debt because if they do, it would lose the interest that went with the loans. Here the vermin's teeth sank deep into the body of the host and drew out a lot of blood from the host into the vermin.

Other conditions of the loans also made lending a paying undertaking for Gebas.

Liberalization of trade and privatization of state industries were some of the conditions Gebas imposed on loans it wanted to grant than those borrowing wanted to borrow. By tricks and subterfuge, Gebas made borrowers think they needed borrowing more than Gebas needed lending. So, they submitted to the draconian conditions Gebas imposed on its loans.

'You can't be rich without tricks and deviousness,' Bongoder said one day to Pettas after council meeting.

'You bet,' Pettas said. Though now a very old man, he had not changed. He was as conscienceless as he was sycophantic. He was the old tortoise that would go to his grave without repenting of his wiliness. Looking at him Bongoder wondered how he became so unconscionable.

'No one has ever been wealthy without tricks here and there; without cheating here and there,' Bongoder continued, his eyes on Pettas. 'Just pray you are not caught.'

Liberalization of trade in the nations Gebas gave loans to allow Gebas flood those nations with its goods. Producing goods, these nations found their goods could not compete with Gebas.' Gebas has been in the business much longer and so could produce the goods cheaper. Producing the goods cheaper, it could undersell new comers into the market. In vain they produced goods they had collected loans to produce – loans they had to pay the interest and the principal. The vermin sank its teeth deeper.

Privatization of public enterprises was one of the conditions imposed by Gebas on loans it granted to poor nations. This allows Gebas to invest its money in other nations thereby taking over the industries of these nations. Investing in these industries, Gebas own the industries and determined what they produced. If it feels what the industries produce would compete with what was produced in Gebas, it would bring down the quality of the products of the industries so that their products could not compete with those of Gebas. If the products of the foreign industries will not compete with products from Gebas, Gebas investors owning these industries would make them produce something of quality which could be profitably sold. When such thing is sold profitably, Gebas investors would collect their dividends and repatriate them to Gebas. When these investors could not get the kind of dividends they envisaged in an enterprise, they divest and take their money home. The vermin pressed on.

'Gebas promoted freedom in politics and economics because it was the beneficiary of these freedoms,' Bongoder said to Gebas' envoy in Bimigan.

'Yes, your majesty,' the envoy said.

'Freedom in politics allows people in poor nations elect their leaders giving them the feeling of being in charge when Gebas is in charge,' Bongoder went on. 'The leaders they elect turn to mere puppets in our hands. Freedom in economics makes for liberalization of trade, and privatization which benefit Gebas than anyone.'

The Kuasee people believe when a tick feeds on an animal for a long time or a bedbug feeds on a human being for a long time, the animal or human being would develop *ping-ping* disease. The *ping-ping* disease makes a person afflicted by it to shrink, cough and gasp for breath. It also develops rashes and boils on the body of the person or animal suffering it.

When Bongoder went to Bimigan on a state visit after thirty years of being on the throne of Gebas, what he met in Bimigan were symptoms of the *ping-ping* disease. It was summer, but the country was literally withering like a tree. Businesses were folding up and social unrest was everywhere. Poverty was walking the tattered streets of the nation in rags making Bongoder wonder if the *ping-ping* disease had also made this nation mad.

Chapter Nine

Sometimes in a rare visitation of conscience, Bongoder used to come hard on himself and Gebas as a nation for the poverty their vermination has caused around the world. If they had not gone round the world taking over what was not theirs, things wouldn't have been this bad in the poor nations of the earth. Vermination was the highland that produce the rivers of problems on earth. During these moments of visitation of conscience, he was often surprised, Gebas' vermination of other nations had not spark off wildcat reprisal attacks from the victims of the vermination.

Lapol was a friend Bongoder used to share his visitation of conscience with whenever it came calling. 'The problems we have with the environment arose from vermination on the environment,' Bongoder said to Lapol on one of his visitations of conscience.

'If we were only living on the environment without greed; if it was only a matter of survival and not wealth accumulation and prosperity, things wouldn't be this bad,' Lapol said.

'The problems we have with poverty, war and hatred around the world has vermination as the highland it flows from,' Bongoder said.

'You can't be more right,' Lapol said. 'My wonder is why we are showing surprise and even pious anger at people we verminated yesterday occasionally bombing us or coming to us looking for jobs – jobs either the wealth of their labour of yesteryears created or resources we looted from them and are still looting from them created.'

Bongoder's visitations of conscience were very brief and spasmodic. Often, he found divine justification for his vermination of other nations. The bible begins by saying everything was created by God for man. From this verse of the bible, man gets divine approval from God to be a vermin on all things on earth. From man verminating on rivers, trees, land and animals, he began verminating on his fellow man. Vermination on human beings was what led to slavery – the appropriation of labour of others for the profit of one.

Though Gebas and other nations started vermination very early, consequences of their vermination did not start rising against them until much later. Much later however, people from countries that had suffered vermination from Gebas and other verminating countries around the world, started moving to the countries that verminated them. The hosts were out of blood and were rushing to the vermins for blood they sucked from them.

The first wave of migrants to Gebas came from Bimigan. According to Bedtam, 'ants work hard. If they can't see what they worked so hard to store up, they will go after those who ate it. The ants are spreading out to the lands of those who ate what they worked for. Migration to foreign lands by migrants from poor nations are all products of vermination.'

Belaru was the victim of Gebas' vermination of his country through free trade. When Bongoder was surprised the vermination of other countries by Gebas had not spark off wildcat reprisal attacks from the victims of vermination, Belaru was on the threshold of launching such attacks.

Chapter Ten

Belaru was the only child of his parents. When he lost his parents at the age of seven, he went to stay with his uncle eking a living from a small restaurant business. The uncle had eight children he was struggling to provide for and Belaru proved one more mouth too many. For days, Belaru would go without much food and without much care. To remain in school, he cut grass to sell to horse owners and fetched water in tins to sell to those who needed it. His determination to remain in school and acquire knowledge was great. This determination saw him through primary school, college and the university. In the university, he read economics. Through his readings, particularly his readings of economic history, he came to understand who killed his father and mother turning him into an orphan at an age he could not provide for himself. He was livid with rage. By more reading, thinking and discussion with friends and course mates, he developed keen insight into political and economic issues and how these issues determine the content of law, politics and education.

One day he and Galla his friend in the university as was common with them were discussing politics and economics in their room in the hostel.

'At the national level, the interest of the ruling class determines the content of law, economics and the educational system,' Belaru said.

'What is a crime and what is not, who gets what and who gets nothing, what is taught in school and what is not taught are all determined by the interest of the ruling class.'

'That's true,' said Galla.

'As the case is in national politics it is in international politics,' Belaru continued. 'The most powerful nations run the show. They determine what you produce and what you don't; how much you sell what you produce and how much you don't sell it; what you privatize and what you keep public.'

'It is quite unfair,' said Galla.

'It is,' said Belaru. 'We as a nation are this poor not necessarily because we have been less frugal or industrious, but because the international metropolitan center has taken wealth from us and given us poverty through free trade, foreign investment and usurious lending. The developed nations are so well off not necessarily because they have been more industrious or frugal, but because they have been able to take wealth from us through free trade, foreign investment and usurious lending.'

'How do they take money from us through free trade to make themselves rich and we poor?' Galla asked.

'Free trade allows them to kill our industries with their goods,' Belaru said with a marked tone of anger. 'Having no goods of our own, we buy theirs. When you buy something from someone, money leaves you and goes to the seller; you become poorer, he becomes richer. By killing our industries, our people are thrown out of jobs and therefore are made poorer. By buying their goods, their people are kept in their jobs and are richer for this. Can you now see how cruelly and evilly the system is skewed to our disadvantage to make us poor and to their advantage to make them rich?'

'I can,' Galla said with a forlorn face.

'They insist on free trade now because their industries have grown, are adults and can beat up infant industries in developing nations. When their industries were infants like ours, they were not talking of free trade. Instead, they were talking of how to protect their industries like the little chicks they were from the hawks circling the skies.'

'Was that so?'

'It was so. When Gebas' textiles were chicks, it banned the importation of fabrics into it. When someone dies, the priest must ascertain the shroud the dead person was to be buried in came from Gebas. If it did not, the person who imported it would have his hand amputated. If he repeated the offence, he was hung.'

'What!'

'That was how hostile Gebas was to free trade when its industries were infants and could not withstand the swooping hawks above. Now that its industries have grown, Gebas is for free trade; its own industries are no more chicks, but the hawks circling the skies. We whose industries are the chicks are arm-twisted and brainwashed into accepting free trade as an economic truth from the god of economics. We are asked to take off our wings from our chicks for the hawks abroad to easily devour them.'

'It is very unfair.'

'Selfish, cruel, evil and wicked are the words. Even when the industries of a developed country are strong and it preaches free trade, whenever the goods of their industries are in danger of not being able to compete well with goods from industries from outside, they abandon free trade and take to protection of their industries. Not long ago Saton passed a law that says its people should buy only tyres made in Saton. Why did it do so? Because Saton tyre companies are finding it difficult to compete with tyre companies from elsewhere.'

'So selfish.'

'Yes, so bloody selfish and self-serving. By free trade, they promote consumption of their goods and services. The more people buy their goods and services around the world, the more they are richer and buyers of their goods and services poorer.'

'These guys surely know how to skin others and scheme themselves into fortunes.'

'They sure do.'

'How do they take money from us through foreign investment to make themselves rich and we poor?'

'Through foreign investment, they own your companies,' Belaru said, his voice slightly rising.

'Owning your companies, they own the profit these companies make and take it to their countries. Again, money leaves you making you poorer and goes to them making them richer.'

'Terrible!' Galla exclaimed.

'Yes, it is terrible,' said Belaru.

'How do they take money from us through lending of money to make themselves rich and we poor?' Galla asked.

'They lend you money and charge heavy interest. You not only repay what was lent to you but heavy interest on it. Often, the interest is much more than what you were lent. Paying interest on loans, money leaves you making you poorer and goes to them making them richer.'

'But they also give us money as aid.'

'You think what you often hear being given to us as aid is free money?' Belaru asked.

'What is it if it is not free money?'

'It is loaned money.'

'You don't mean it?'

'I mean it.'

'Why then are they calling it aid?'

'They call it aid because it is given to you when you need it, or think you need it, or have been made to think you need it. It is also aid because it is usually at a lower interest rate than you can get elsewhere in the lending market.'

'God will punish them,' Galla swore panting with hate.

'Amen. Unfortunately, God will not punish them because he is always on the side of the strongest army and they are the strongest army,' Belaru said with haunting sarcasm.

'God always on the side of the strongest army?'

'That's what Napoleon Bonaparte said and that's what I see.'

'Terrible.'

'Yes, terrible. But don't worry. One day we will punish them,' Belaru said with a revolutionary tone of voice. 'This iniquitous system for sure cannot be sustained forever. Justice one day will rise up against it.'

'But why does our government accept free trade, foreign investment and loaned money knowing these to be so harmful?'

'Might is right,' Belaru answered. 'Our people are brainwashed and arm-twisted into taking poison as medicine. As they were forced to accept foreign religions and foreign gods as the true religions and gods, they have been brainwashed and forced to accept foreign economic ideas as the truth. In fact, any of us who seeks to show these economic ideas are not good for us is looked at with contempt by his own people who had been brainwashed to believe in the ideas.'

'It is sad.'

'It is indeed sad,' Belaru said. 'There's also the issue of …'

'No, no, no Belaru; I can't take any more,' Galla interrupted Belaru holding his head with both hands and blocking his ears. 'Already my head is swelling with anger from what I had taken. If I take any more of this stuff something bad will happen to me or to someone. Maybe tomorrow we can continue the discourse, not any more today.'

'That's OK,' Belaru said. 'Tomorrow then.'

Chapter Eleven

Belaru and Galla could not meet to continue their discussion the following day as they agreed because Belaru had to travel out of school to attend to his cousin who was sick. It was after a week the two men were able to meet again. That was when Belaru returned.

'You stayed too long, what happened?'

'Man, that boy is very sick,' Belaru said, looking depressed. 'If care is not taken, we may lose him, and he is about the only close relation I have of my age.'

'Then care has to be taken,' Galla said.

'Unfortunately, the means we need to take care do not exist in this country,' Belaru said with a forlorn look.

'What do you mean?' Galla asked.

'There are no hospitals any more in the country. If you are seriously sick, you have to be flown abroad or you die.'

'Our situation is quite unfortunate,' Galla said, dejectedly.

'It is. Medical care is now only for the rich who have money to fly their sick ones abroad for treatment, and how many are the rich people that can afford this?' Belaru lamented

'Very few,' Galla said.

'Yes, very few, and this is because of the prevalence of poverty which we were discussing the day before I traveled. Without jobs, our people are poor. My uncle – my cousin's father, has been out of work for three years. He cannot even afford good medical treatment for his son in this country. Talking of flying him out for treatment is like mocking him.'

'But we can hardly blame anyone for the conditions of our hospitals,' Galla said. 'It is all due to the corruption of our leaders. Instead of using the little money we have to fix our hospitals, they steal it, and here we are without hospitals.'

'You are right blaming the corruption of our leaders for the condition of our hospitals,' said Belaru. 'But this corruption of our leaders in some way is promoted by commissions they are paid for borrowing money from international financial institutions or from developed nations' banks.'

'I don't understand.'

'You see, if a country borrows money from an international financial institution like the World Bank or the International Monetary Fund, the leader of the nation that borrowed the money is given a commission for bringing a client who will pay a lot of interest on the loan he had been given.'

'What!'

'That's how it is. Also, one of the conditions of the loan when its repayment becomes difficult will likely be that the country should reduce its expenditure on healthcare, housing or education – the so-called unproductive and unprofitable sectors of the economy. The money saved from reduction of expenditure on healthcare, housing and education is then used to service the country's debts if they cannot be repaid,' Belaru said. 'This way money meant for healthcare is diverted to servicing debts killing our hospitals.'

'This is terrible.'

'Annoying is the word.'

'This debt servicing, what is it all about?'

'It is all about payment of interests on loans and not repaying the loans themselves.'

'This is terrible,'

'Infuriating is the word.'

'God will punish them.'

'No, we will punish them,' said Belaru with verve. 'God is too busy for this and the matter is too petty for him.'

'The matter is too petty for him?'

'Yes, it is too petty for him. We go about saying God will punish someone, God will bless someone as if God has no work but going around blessing and punishing people. We have made God so petty. I wonder when the holy writs say we are made in the image of God, there's a design in this to make God suffer our pettiness.'

'What!'

'Yes.'

'Well, let's leave God alone and talk about our troubles.'

'Yes, our troubles, particularly our troubles with healthcare,' Belaru said. 'Traditional medicine from which we would have been getting treatment has almost completely disappeared. Bio-piracy is taking the traditional medicine knowledge of our people and vesting it in big pharmaceutical corporations of developed nations.'

'I don't understand.'

'Before the so-called modern era, our people had knowledge of traditional medicine, which, at a low or no cost, they used to heal our people of common and rare ailments,' Belaru said. 'The same way folk story tellers passed on folk tales, our traditional medicine men passed on their knowledge of traditional medicine to their offspring, which the offspring, like their forbears before them, used to heal their generation of common and rare ailments also at a low or no cost. The traditional medicine knowledge of our people is now being taken over by big pharmaceutical corporations of developed nations whose drugs carry prohibitive price tags. Pharmaceutical companies of developed countries regularly identify traditional knowledge from healers in Africa and Asia, patent it in the west and reap the profits of their monopoly in high cost of medical care. For instance, traditional Samoan healers have for generations been grinding up the stem of the *Homolanthusacuminatus* plant, steeping it in hot water as a treatment for viral infections. This traditional medicine knowledge of the Samoan healers has been pirated, stolen by a Saton pharmaceutical corporation and has been patented for the corporation. By patenting this knowledge for the corporation, it is western pharmaceutical companies, not the Samoan government or people, who will profit from the millions made from sales of the viral infection drugs the pirated Samoan healers' knowlege was used to produce. In Peru, maca the high-altitude plant with a reputation as a fertility enhancer has been grown for centuries by indigenous people who used it to enhance fertility in men as in women. Despite its popular traditional use, a predatory Saton corporation filed and got a patent granted to it on the plant's natural viagra properties. Similarly, the hoodia plant of the Kalahari Desert long used by so-called Bushmen on long journeys because it helps stave off hunger pangs has been patented for a pharmaceutical corporation of a developed nation for its potential as a diet drug.'

'This is wicked,' Galla interjected.

'Criminal is the word,' Belaru said.

'Yet on a second thought, I feel our people with knowledge of traditional medicine are as guilty on this matter as the pharmaceutical companies of developed nations that steal their knowledge,' Galla said after a while of thoughtful silence.

'How?' Belaru asked with an expression that looked like one of surprise.

'For not passing on their knowledge to their offspring.'

'How can they pass on what has been stolen?' Belaru said with an amused expression on his face.

Galla laughed. 'Belaru, you are a bad case,' he said.

'I hear you,' Belaru chuckled.

'Jokes aside,' Galla said after a while of silence, 'Belaru, why do our people with knowledge of traditional medicine do not pass it to their offspring? Why do they allow it to be stolen by pharmaceutical companies of developed nations?'

'Yes, jokes aside,' Belaru said, peremptorily. 'You know how things have always been with our people,' he went on in a somber tone. 'They are naive, too simple, and generous with knowledge. Rarely do they think of making money from their knowledge. As they easily pass on knowledge to their offspring without a fee, they do so to strangers.'

'It is sad.'

'It is indeed sad,' Belaru said in a haunting voice. 'You also know as I do that our people have been manipulated and brainwashed by so-called modern medicine practitioners and sponsors to despise traditional medicine. Finding fewer patronizers and fewer offspring to pass their knowledge of traditional medicine to, owners of knowledge of traditional medicine pass it to anyone interested. The person interested is often a pharmaceutical company of a deveoped nation. Modern medicine has done to traditional medicine what free trade did to the textitle company my father worked in. It has killed it.'

'It is sad.'

'It is indeed sad.' Belaru said poised to continue his exposition of a situation he thought unjust. 'After taking over the traditional medicine knowledge of indigenous people in developing nations, pharmaceutical corporations of developed nations also take over the biological resources of developing nations through genetic modification technology. For instance, the pharmaceutical corporation Eli Lily owned by a developed nation has developed two cancer drugs from the rosy periwinkle of Madagascar. Eli Lily has made hundreds of millions of dollars from the drugs. The people of Madagascar on the other hand have gained nothing. Pharmaceutical companies argue that biological resources like the rosy periwinkle of Madagascar should be treated as common resources and so they owe nothing to Madagascar or its people. The government and people of Madagascar and many other communities around the world on the other hand have argued that the resulting drugs are not treated as common resources. On the contrary, the drugs are well protected by intellectual property rights as the property of the corporation that produced the drugs from the plant.

Modification of plant and animal genetics by use of bio-technology also provides opportunity to bio-technology corporations of developed nations for bio-piracy. By plants genetic modification, bio-technology corporations of developed countries change the genetics of plants and patent the genetically modified plants for themselves. For instance, the genetics of guavas, mangoes, oranges, apples and sugarcane have all been modified by bio-technology corporations of developed countries which now owned such genetically modified plants through patents granted to them over the plants. Owning genetically modified guavas, mangoes, oranges, apples and sugarcane, they are paid royalties for the fruits of these plants sold around the world. As it is with plants, it is with animals. Chickens and fishes have been genetically modified by bio-technology corporations of developed nations and are now owned by the corporations that genetically modified them. Owning genetically modified chickens and fishes, they are paid royalties on such chickens and fishes sold around the world.

In particular, patenting of plants for bio-technology corporations is an attempt to rob developing countries in the south of genetic wealth they have in excess of what developed nations of the north have. It is known by every informed mind that the southern hemisphere is far more ecologically rich than the northern hemisphere. What genetic modification seeks to do is to enable corporations from the developed countries of the north to appropriate the genetic wealth of the south which the south then has to pay for.'

'This is terrible!' Galla exclaimed, panting with hate.

'Enraging is the word,' Belaru said. 'To ensure their corporations get away with theft, developed nations with big pharmaceutical corporations work tirelessly and viciously to ensure patents granted to their corporations over stolen or pirated pharmaceutical knowledge or resources from developing nations are protected by international law. This is what Trade-Related Aspects of Intellectual Property Rights – TRIPS, is all about. To a shameless and embarrassing extent, the Saton Government fought to ensure that poor developing nations sign TRIPS to legitimise the theft of their resources.

'This is very infuriating,' Galla said in an abject tone.

'As infuriating as the action of Saton is, the nonchallance of the governments of developing nations to the plight of their people whose knowledge of traditional medicine is being stolen by pharmaceutical corporations of developed nations is more infuriating and contemptible,' Belaru continued. 'While governments of developed nations fight for their pharmaceutical corporations to protect their theft which brings wealth to their nations, governments of developing nations do nothing to protect or even support the protest and struggles of their traditional medicine knowledge owners against the theft of their intellectual property.'

'But how can they be protesting the takeover of their knowledge by the pharmaceutical companies after willingly parting with it to them?' Galla interposed.

'Apparently some, if not all of them, have realized their folly,' Belaru said.

'This sounds salutary.'

'Yes, it does. What however is not salutary is the attitude of the governments of developing nations to the protest of their people. Instead of the governments of these nations seeing the wealth of their traidtional medicine knowledge owners as their own wealth and fight for them the same way developed nations see the wealth of their pharmaceutical companies as their own wealth and fight for them, the former don't see the matter in this light. So they allow their traditional medicine knowledge owners to fight their own war without any form of support from them. How can the antelope fight the hyena without at least the support of the wolf? The Letico and Kimberley Declarations in which traditional medicine knowledge owners asserted their rights to their knowledge have been made, but of what consequence are they compared to TRIPS?

'This is really biting,' Galla mourned.

With TRIPS, Saton's aspirations to own ideas and images has been fulfilled,' Belaru went on.

'Own ideas and images?'

'Yes, own ideas and images,' Belaru said. 'Since the 1980s, Saton has been pursuing a policy of de-industrialization. Under this policy, dirty, polluting industries were forced to leave Saton for developing countries. That was how *Bedes* companies came to populate Lakuk. That is how Lakuk is suffering pollution and Saton is free of it. Owning ideas and images in the forms of patents and trademarks, royalties are paid to Saton without it producing anything.'

'What!'

'This is how it is,' Belaru said. 'By the way, people who invented monotheistic religions did a similar thing much earlier: They own *divine ideas and images* in the forms of *God and holy sites* for which they are paid royalties through pilgrimages and purchase of religious artefacts and talismans.'

'You are not serious.'

'I can't be more serious.'

'But why do our governments and people accept these unfair and wicked schemes that make them terribly worse off?' asked Galla in a painful voice.

'Yes, why do our governments and people accept to live with these nasty and unfair conditions?' Belaru enthused. 'Ignorance,' he went on in a rabid tone. 'Acceptance of the current unfair world order is mostly because of ignorance. People in poor developing nations do not know that what nature gave them free is being taken over by greedy corporations of developed nations who they now have to pay money to. Crippled by ignorance, people in poor developing nations cannot link their poverty and misery to the wealth and happiness of developed nations. They don't understand that they are made poor and miserable so that others can be rich and happy.

'This again is getting too much for me to bear,' Galla said, holding his head with both hands.

'Again, my head is swelling as it did the other day. I can't take any more of this.'

'We continue another day then,' Belaru said, getting up from where he had been sitting and talking.

'See you later,' Galla said already walking away. 'When I can take more, I will see you.'

Chapter Twelve

Two days later, Galla went to Belaru's hostel looking a little disoriented and flustered. Belaru, on seeing him wondered what the matter was with his friend. 'What is biting you?' he asked.

'It is so difficult making sense out of life,' Galla said.

'Ha ha ha!' Belaru issued a mirthless laughter.

'Why are you laughing?'

'Because you spoke as if you just came to the world,' Belaru said. 'As someone who has been around, you should have known long ago that it is difficult making sense of life.'

'I have long known it is difficult making sense of life. But things keep happening that force you into saying what I just said.'

'You are right,' Belaru said. 'That we all know there's death does not make us less shocked or sorrowful when someone dear to us dies.'

'You see what I mean.'

'Something happened, and a man said God is wonderful. Another man on hearing him asked him if he was just discovering the wonderfulness of God. The first man said he had always known God is wonderful, but something had happened that made him make the exclamation.'

'You see what I mean.'

'I not only see what you mean, it speaks to me.'

Galla laughed.

'Jokes apart, what made you say what you said?'

'Some days ago, you almost convinced me free trade is a demon,' Galla said.

'So, I only almost,' Belaru said with a mild look of disappointment. 'I thought I convinced you free trade is not only a demon but the devil himself. It is so difficult knowing whether you have convinced anyone or not.'

Galla chuckled. 'Indeed, you convinced me free trade is both the devil and Satan. But I just read somewhere that free trade ended feudalism in Gebas,' he said after a while of silence.

'Interesting,' Belaru said in a tranquil tone. 'How?'

'Free trade produced merchants that bought the land of the so-called noblemen.'

'So, the merchants became the new noblemen,' Belaru said with a tinge of sarcasm.

'No, there were no more noblemen.'

'That would have been wonderful,' Belaru quipped.

'And so it is,' Galla intoned.

'I know something about feudalism in Gebas and what killed it if indeed it was killed,' Belaru said in a grave tone. 'I have read about the three estates of feudalism in Gebas: the bellatores – noblemen who exploited the poor, the laboratores – the poor who tilled the land and worked the mills for miserly emoluments, and the oratores –

clergymen who kept the poor from revolting. I have also been told by books how merchants bought so-called noblemen out of their land. But I don't think this was what ended feudalism in Gebas if indeed it was ended. I think it was Black Death that seriously reversed the fortunes of feudalism in Gebas as elsewhere in Europe.'

'Black Death?'

'Yes, Black Death – the so-called bubonic plague spread by black rats.'

'How did Black Death end feudalism?'

'Feudalism thrives on cheap labor. Many poor people who provided cheap labor were killed by the bubonic plague. Because of their death, the so-called noblemen could no longer have access to cheap labor that generated so much wealth for them. Faced with dwindling fortunes, they began selling their land to the merchants you are talking about. The merchants more interested in trading in land than cultivating it, had less use for the laboratores who were thus freed from their sweatshops. Both the laborers and the merchants – the parvenu, were beneficiaries of Black Death.'

'What?'

'Yes. It was the death of the kith and kin of the laborers in the bubonic plague that freed them from their labor.'

'What an awry and bizarre turn of events! Death freeing people?'

'Yes, death freeing people. Because of his selfish and self-seeking nature, things will always be bizarre with man.'

'It is so disappointing.'

'With his selfishness and self-seeking character, things with man will always be disappointing. Initially, it was thought a spirit of benevolence in mankind led to the end of slavery.'

'It didn't?'

'It didn't.'

'What did?'

'The slaves and the steam engine.'

'The slaves and the steam engine? What do you mean?'

'Slaves' labor in the plantations produced surplus agricultural products that needed to be processed if they would not waste. So slave owners started thinking of what to do to avoid waste. Their thinking led them to producing the steam engine. The steam engine led to production of more goods. There was no more need for slave labor. So, slavery had to be abolished. Again, the goods produced by the steam engine needed to be sold, but there were only few buyers. Slaves that would have increased the number of buyers had no money because they are not paid for their labor. So, they were freed to work and be paid money they would use to buy the goods produced by the steam engine.'

'Incredible!'

'Unfortunately, it is true. There's no do-gooder in the world.'

'Slaves and the steam engine ending slavery?'

'That was what happened.'

'It is so difficult knowing what is what.'

'Yes, it is so difficult knowing what is what.

'Not only is it difficult making sense of life, it is difficult knowing what is true and what is a lie.'

'That's also true,' Belaru said with what looked like a faint smile on his lips. 'That's why you shouldn't be in a hurry to die for what you think is the truth. You may find out after your death that you died for a lie.'

'You are not serious,' Galla said, laughing.

'I wish I am not.'

'It is so painfully pricking.'

'Yes, it is. With so much selfishness and ignorance about, it is so difficult knowing what is what.'

'The other day you spoke of ignorance; now you are speaking of it again,' Galla said with an awaken sense of enthusiasm.

'Ignorance makes people see the oppressor as a do-gooder when they should see him as the bad guy he is. Why, for instance, should the laity respect the clergy when the clergy as oratores hold them down as laboratores to be exploited by the bellatores – the so-called noblemen? But for ignorance, the laity should be hanging knives on the throats of the clergy every day. But what do you see? Ignorance makes the victim revere his tormentor. It makes him put up with an unfair economic system that robs

Peter to pay Paul. It prevents people in poor developing nations from seeing it is their wealth that makes the developed nations rich; that it is their poverty that is feeding their masters.'

Chapter Thirteen

'The other day you were blaming ignorance for our docility against an unjust international socio-economic order,' Galla said when he and Belaru met again. 'Who do you think is responsible for this ignorance?'

'Those the ignorance feeds,' Belaru said.

'Who are they?'

'The developed nations that own and control big multinational corporations that exploit poor developing nations,' Belaru said.

'How are they able to do this?' Galla asked.

'Mostly through our educational system,' Belaru said.

'Through our educational system? This is strange. Education should be a means of dispelling ignorance, not foisting it,' Galla said with an expression of surprise on his face.

'No doubt, education is supposed to be a vehicle of enlightenment,' Belaru said. 'Unfortunately, this is not what our educational system is. Instead of being a tool of enlightenment, it is skewed to perpetuate ignorance.'

'How?'

'Economics in our educational system for example does not tell us that free trade is good for a developed country, but bad for us. Instead, it tells us that free trade is good for everyone. This is perpetuation of ignorance,' Belaru said. 'It gives the impression that foreign aid is free money when in fact it is loaned money on which interest is paid and the principal is repaid. This is perpetuation of ignorance.'

'It is indeed,' said Galla.

'After foisting and perpetuating ignorance through our educational system, law and religion are fraudulently used to legitimize an unfair, wicked and inhuman system,' Belaru continued after a momentary silence.

'But law is supposed to be a means of giving justice to the people,' said Galla. 'How is it an instrument for perpetrating injustice?'

'Law affirms the unfair international socio-economic order and lends itself to enforcing it,' said Belaru. 'For instance, law approves of free trade as good for everyone, approves of lending with usurious interest rate and approves of patenting pirated traditional pharmaceutical knowledge for big pharmaceutical corporations in the name of protection of intellectual property. The law, like God, sides with the strong against the weak, the cheat against the cheated. The law is complicit in the crime against the poor. It is an accessory after the fact of theft and cheating.'

'This is serious.'

'Yes, it is. You see back in my father's village, it was a sinful thing to study law and lawyers were believed never to make heaven. As a younger person when I was told the attitude of my father's people to studying law and being a lawyer, I laughed it off as borne by ignorance. Not anymore.

Now I think their attitude was an uncanny reaction to the iniquitous character of law.'

'You cannot be serious.'

'Unfortunately, I am.'

'Well, let's leave law for now; how is religion an instrument for perpetrating injustice?'

'Religion assists law in its insidious brigandage against the weak and cheated. 'Whatever law fails to legitimize, religion does. Religion makes people accept their poor, miserable conditions as divine. So shackled, they can't rise up against the cheat and thief.'

'So religion and law are partners in crime?'

'They sure are. Religion not only assists law to keep people cheated and exploited, it assists mainstream economic ideas of free trade, foreign investment and borrowing for development.'

'How?'

'Using the same method religion uses to foist religious dogma and superstition on people, mainstream economists from developed nations foist economic dogmas of the goodness of free trade, foreign investment and borrowing money to develop on poor developing nations.

'So religion is also a partner in crime with mainstream economics?'

'It sure is.'

'This is something.'

'No doubt, it is.'

Chapter Fourteen

Shortly before their graduation from university, Belaru and Galla, out for a walk one evening, came by the university's botanical garden. The garden was newly set up by the department of botany to serve as a laboratory for its students. When Belaru and Galla came by the garden, Galla who was studying biology stopped walking to regard a guava tree in the garden closely. 'This tree is developing very fast,' he said.

'What do you mean the tree is developing fast?' Belaru asked in a high pitch voice that communicated excitement and curiosity.

'Well, I mean it is growing very fast,' Galla said, briskly.

'Yes, I thought that was the right term to use in the first place,' said Belaru, his voice falling to its normal pitch.

'On the contrary it is not,' said Galla. 'The right term to use is *developing*, not growing. I only used the term growing because you seem to have a problem with the term *developing*.'

'This is interesting,' Belaru said, excitement returning to his voice and expression.

Galla was intrigued. He rarely saw his friend so excited. Always taciturn, Belaru seemed beyond humor of any kind. Why was he so excited over what he just said? he asked Belaru.

'I have never associated the term *development* with the growth of plants,' Belaru said, losing nothing of his excitement. 'I have always thought of *development* in relation to towns, cities and nations.'

'Knowing who you are, I can't see why this will make you this excited,' Galla said.

'Sure, without more, it will not make me so excited,' Belaru said. 'But there's more. In truth, is *development* the biological term for plant growth or you merely used the term offhandedly?'

'In truth, *development* is the biological term for plant and animal growth,' Galla said in a voice rippling with seriousness. '*Development* refers to an evolutionary process by which a plant or animal attains genetic maturity and bears the fruits it is capable of.'

'Wonderful!' Belaru exclaimed, quite elated. 'In economics, the term *development* is so pervasive it might be said to be one of the cornerstones of the subject. All streams and rivers of economics lead to the sea of *development*. All economic activities are carried out with a view of achieving *development*. Yet from what you just said which makes a lot of sense to me, we borrowed the term from you guys.'

'Without doubt, you did, and you are not paying interest on your loan,' Galla said, pertly.

They both laughed.

'Well, maybe originally we borrowed the term from you, but we later annexed it. Now it belongs more to us than to you. The lawyers have what they call laches and acquiescence. They also have what they call notorious possession. You have lost *development* to us first by laches and acquiescence; then by notorious possession. It now looks like if you want to use the term, you have to borrow it from us and pay the interest.'

Again, they both laughed.

'Why do you guys want to disinherit us?' Galla asked feigning anger.

'Because you are sleeping over your rights,' Belaru said, wryly. 'From ancient times, you can be dispossessed of your inheritance if you sleep over it. Now, we see it happening every day. Even what you know can be taken from you and given to another person and you may have to buy from that person an article he used your knowledge to produce. This is what happens in bio-piracy and patenting of drugs for pharmaceutical companies who either pirated our knowledge of herbal medicine or pirated the genetic resources of our plants.'

'You are right,' Galla said. 'The most perverse things happen in the world today and life goes on as if nothing is happening.'

'There you are,' Belaru said, fervently.

'Ours is indeed an unjust, greedy and gluttonous world,' Galla said after an interval of silence.

'There you are,' Belaru said, rabidly. 'Perhaps in only few areas of human life do you see this greed and gluttony manifesting themselves than in the area of plants *development*. In the perverse economics of *development*, guava develops when it is genetically modified to produce big guava fruits. So are mangoes, so is sugar cane. Food engineering today is about engineering plants and animals to be high-yielding or to be producing fatter fruits than their evolution makes allowance for. However, tragically, and perhaps unavoidably, food high-yielding engineering often engineers diseases that are high-yielding in death. Our stomachs may always be full, but they are full with genetically modified high-yielding feeds that breed disease and death.'

Galla laughed in spite of himself. 'Feeds! Are we chickens and fishes?'

'Today there's no much difference between what we are fed with and what chickens and fishes are fed with. We are all agro-chickens and fishes. We grow alike, look alike and die alike of common ailments.'

'So awful and pathetic.'

'Yes, so dreadful and pitiful. But the development ideology and food high-yielding engineering press on. Every country must develop and produce fruits or it suffers the curse of the fig tree.'

Again, Galla laughed.

'At the heart of the problems of so-called developing nations is the concept of *development*. Like an IMF loan, what we economists borrowed from you the biologists, is neither helping us nor the world,' Belaru said.

'Belaru, you are a bad case,' Galla said in an uproarious laughter.

'If you are a developing nation, you have to borrow money and take foreign investment to develop. Meanwhile, to be able to eat what the developed world is eating, to have a high standard of living, you have to open your borders to free trade.'

'We are caught up in a snowballing mess,' Galla said.

'Without doubt, we are.'

'High standard of living; that's another one,' Galla remarked, somberly.

'Yes, it is another culprit and in fact the biggest culprit,' Belaru said with renewed verve. 'It is obsession with so-called high standard of living that generated the thirst and hunger to develop in the first place. So, high standard of living is the progenitor of *development. Development* is a mere protégé driven to action by high standard of living.'

'The whole thing is as rotten as it is fascinating,' Galla remonstrated.

'It is,' intoned Belaru. 'When you are called a developing nation, that designation forces you into a race to catch up, to develop. This benefits the person that has christened you a developing nation because you have to buy his goods and services to develop. With all the mirrors around, today you don't see yourself; others see you and tell you who you are. You don't know yourself; someone knows you. You don't know what is good for you;

someone knows what is good for you. I thought even a cow knows the grass that is good for it.'

'It is both phony and funny,' Galla said in an acidic tone. 'The whole concept of *development* in economics is politics from root to branch.'

'It is,' rejoined Belaru. 'Maybe I should have read natural science like biology. There's less politics and lies in natural science. Social science is a horse of a different color altogether. It is so full of fraud. Law is fraud; economics is fraud; politics is fraud. I have always suspected social science of the same dubiety I suspect religion of.'

'Is religion itself not a social science?'

'Yes and no. To the extent that religion is something authority invented after studying human nature and tendencies, yes, religion is a social science. To the extent religion is absurd to intelligence, reason and commonsense, no, religion is not a social science but petty superstition.'

'Well, whatever it is, I think it is good you are reading economics,' Galla said. 'Reading and knowing the lies of social science empowers you to fight the system.'

'You are surely saying something there,' Belaru said. 'Reading economics has helped me know there is nothing absolute about economics. The science is a relative one. *Ceteris paribus* explains the whole of economics. What you do and succeed or fail depends on your situation. There are no hard and fast rules in economics. Everything is in a state of flux in this science. The working or not working of anything in economics depends on many things holding together or not holding together; on variables hanging together to make it work or not hanging together to make it fail. Reading this science has helped me understand thoroughly the living fraud called the international economic order breathing disaster around the world.

'The concept of *development* in economics is both satanic and demonic,' Galla said after a moment of silence.

'Without doubt it is.'

'The harm it causes calls for someone's head.'

'True; it does call for the cheating and thieving heads of some people.'

Chapter Fifteen

After school, Belaru worked briefly in a manufacturing company but was laid off because the company was scaling down its operations due to declining demands for its products. Later, he got a lecturing job in a university. Hardly did he leave a class without telling his students that the world should say farewell to peace if it insists on sustaining the current unjust socio-economic order.

After fifteen years of teaching, he was sacked for teaching students what he was not paid to teach.

'I am not teaching what I am paid to teach?' he asked the Vice Chancellor after receiving his sack letter.

'Yes, you are not.'

'What am I paid to teach that I am not teaching?'

'You are paid to teach economics. From reports reaching me, you are not teaching this subject; instead, you are teaching politics.'

'This is preposterous. Who told you I am teaching politics?' Belaru asked, aghast.

'Your students and other lecturers.'

'So, my students and colleagues report on me.'

'Not only on you, but on every other lecturer.'

'What, if I may ask, is the economics I am supposed to teach, and the politics I am not supposed to teach?' Belaru asked.

'The economics you are supposed to teach are the theories and principles of economics. The politics you are not supposed to teach are how certain economic theories and practices work to exploit or pauperize some and enrich others.'

'You call the type of economics you want me to teach economics?'

'What do you call it?'

'Perpetuation of ignorance.'

'Call it what you like. Someone is paying for the sustenance of this institution. He does not like what you are teaching.'

'By someone you mean the government?'

'Yes, I mean the government.'

'The puppet government you mean?'

'Call it what you like; it pays the piper and therefore dictates the tune.'

'Well, this piper cannot be dictated to.'

'So, he should go. This university can ill-afford the presence of dissident scholars like you.'

Belaru saw his sack as the handiwork of those who want education in poor developing nations to be an instrument of perpetuating ignorance. Even before his sack, he had long decided to mobilize like-minded people for an attack on the international socio-economic order that was so unfair. So, when he was sacked, he formed the Tendu-Purgers with the Sekia Mountains as their operational headquarters. Their mission was to purge the world of socio-economic injustice.

Every Tendu-Purger was trained to be a marksman, a bomber and a leader. Every purger could not only lead an operation, he could lead the movement. With every one as leader, the insurgent group could not be decapitated by killing Belaru who they called the grand commander. With every purger schooled in the science and art of leadership, marksmanship and bombing, they were sure to be more effective and invincible. The war cry of the purgers was:

> Hit those who sustain the system!
> Hit those who benefit from the system!
> Bomb the system!
> What the world needs is fairness, not charity.
> Let's be fair to everyone.
> And there will be no need for so-called charity.

Every day Belaru moved around looking for people to recruit into Tendu-Purgers. Usually, he knew who to recruit after discussing with the person and ascertaining his position on international socio-economic injustice in the world. That was how he recruited Dakas whom he was now taking to the Sekia Mountains.

Chapter Sixteen

In a big cave in the Sekia Mountains was a squad of Tendu-Purgers jubilating over a victory they just had over a platoon of the Blufor army. The young purger who led the attack was at the center of the purgers being mobbed by fellow purgers for a good job. They were all reliving and relishing the success of the surprise attack in which they wiped out a whole platoon of the Blufor army without losing any of their members. The attack was sudden, decisive and surgical. The platoon was caught off guard and before it could recover from the shock of the attack, it was all over. All the platoon members were dead – cut down by bullets of the Tendu-Purgers. The Tendu-Purgers melted into the treacherous tunnels and caves of the Sekia Mountains in jubilation.

It was in their jubilant state that Belaru and his new recruit met them when they got to the Sekia mountains. As the two men made their way into the cave, they could hear the purgers speaking randomly:

'They can't say they didn't expect what we gave them after the raw deals they have been serving us.'

'They can't even say we are not fair to them, can they?'

'Beneficiaries of the flatulence of injustice moved about with paunches while the rest of us moved about with empty bowels.'

'All those carrying sacks in front of them would be rid of their sacks. It is in those sacks they carry the commonwealth.'

Then the two men just arriving the cave heard the war cry:

Hit those who sustain the system!
Hit those who benefit from the system!
Bomb the system!
What the world needs is fairness, not charity.
Let's be fair to everyone.
And there will be no need for so-called charity.

'What is the celebration for?' Belaru asked when he and Dakas got to the jubilant purgers.

'We have just recorded an impressive victory against the system,' the young purger who led the attack said. He went on to give Belaru the details of the attack and how successful it was.

Impressive as this victory was, if Belaru was happy, not much of his happiness showed on his face. He had a fixed unhappy outlook on life that was rarely affected by any happy occurrence or happiness of people around him. The victory was good, but it was a drop that could not dilute his sea of unhappiness over the cheating of the weak by the strong and stealing of resources of developing nations by developed nations.

With little show of excitement, he congratulated his fellow purgers for a good job and introduced Dakas as a new purger.

'You are welcome,' the old purgers said without much scrutiny of Dakas. They trusted the judgment of the grand commander. He would not recruit a traitor of the cause.

After introducing Dakas, Belaru produced a world map from his pocket and sat down to pore over it. Every purger except Dakas knew what he was poring over the map for. He was looking for their next target of attack. After poring over the map for a long while, he identified the target. He signified this by groaning and tapping a spot on the map with his fingers. It was the World Trade Foundation in Comin.

'Our next target is the World Trade Foundation in Comin,' he declared. 'It is from there they export poverty to us.'

All the purgers ululated in happiness.

'In the pit of their greed, death awaits those who cheat others ...,' Belaru spat.

'We are that death,' the purgers enthused.

'As we sit in the pit of this mountain, we are sitting in the pit of their greed…'

'And will strike without pity.'

'Fair trade that would have been just was frustrated by unjust free trade...'

'How about free death?'

'You give us fair life …'
'We give you fair life.'
'You give us free death …'
'We give you free death.
'Heirs of the system …'
'Breed heirs of war.'
'They are heirs of the system...'
'We are heirs of war.
'They bred us …'
'And must accept responsibility for our actions.'
'The world suffers flatulence of injustice ...'
'It is time it begins to purge.
'For too long it has been farting …'
'And belching to our offence.'
'When the world said farewell to justice …'
'It said farewell to peace.'
Outside the cave, the sun had climbed over the mountain range and now shone over Sekia forest in all its glory

Chapter Seventeen

Tendu-Purgers had their armory under Sekia Mountains. The flash-striker was their most destructive bomb. They used rocket launchers produced by them to deliver it at distances of four to five kilometers.

Belaru got the funds to acquire the armory from Akkub a rich Oklan with sympathy for developing nations. Akkub inherited the money from his father who was a business magnet with vast business interests in energy and communication industries. Not only did Akkub give Tendu-Purgers the money to acquire the armory, he funded some of their activities.

It was a chance meeting at a conference in Saton that brought Belaru and Akkub together. Belaru delivered a paper on the politics of international economics at the conference. Akkub was impressed by the scholarly quality of the paper and sought audience with Belaru after the conference.

'You seem to have fundamental differences with the system,' Akkub said in a meeting with Belaru after the conference.

'Yes, I have fundamental differences with the system,' Belaru said.

'I do also,' said Akkub.

'You do?' Belaru asked, his eyes popping out with surprise. 'But you are from Okla, a child and beneficiary of the system; a seemingly well circumstanced man of the system.'

'Yes, I am from Okla and no doubt a beneficiary of the system; a well circumstanced man of the system,' Akkub said. 'But we are talking of moral and conscience issues. One's position on these issues is not necessarily determined by his nationality or his personal financial circumstances.'

'You are right,' Belaru said, touched by what Akkub had said.

'Good,' Akkub said. 'So, I as a beneficiary of the system can resent it as much as you, a victim of it.'

'Perhaps yes,' Belaru said.

'Certainly yes,' Akkub said. 'To prove to you I am as against the injustice of the system as you are, I will partner with you on any scheme you propose to redress the injustices in the system.'

After this conversation, the two men exchanged telephone and email contacts. In the course of time, their visions on how to deal with the unjust international socio-economic order united into a firm commitment for changing the world socio-economic order. This was how Akkub came to fund the Tendu-Purgers.

Before carrying out the attack on the World Trade Foundation in Comin, the Tendu-Purgers carried out a reconnaissance survey of the center using pleasure low-flying aircraft fitted with surveillance devices that could see through walls and roofs and high-definition video cameras that could pick pins.

The pictures taken by the cameras were analyzed by Tendu-Purgers video decipherers to determine with precision what was in the trade foundation.

After deciphering the video footages, the decipherers briefed Belaru and the operational unit that would carry out the attack. 'There are five departments in the World Trade Foundation,' Deco the head of video enciphers began. 'They are world trade promotion, trade agreement registry, trade agreement documentation, world trade profile and trade dispute settlement department.'

'Can you show us the precise locations of these departments in the building?' Belaru asked.

'Of course, yes,' said Deco. 'The world trade promotion department is on the third floor of the eastern wing of the building, precisely on this spot,' he continued placing a long ruler he was holding on the spot he said the trade promotion department was. 'The trade agreement registry is on the western wing of the building on the fourth floor, precisely on this spot,' he went on again tapping the spot he said the trade registry department was on the video footage. 'The trade agreement documentation and the world trade profile departments are both on the eastern wing on the fifth floor of the building,' he said again tapping where the two departments were. 'The dispute settlement department is on the western wing of the building on the sixth floor. This is where it is,' he said and tapped where the department was on the video footage.

'Now tell us what is in these various departments you have just shown us,' Belaru said.

'The world trade promotion department is where world trade policy matters and regulations are kept,' Deco continued. 'The trade registry department is where all trade agreements between nations are registered. The register reflecting these agreements is kept in this department. The trade agreement documentation is where copies of the various trade agreements are kept while the world trade profile department keeps statistics of world trade. The dispute settlement department is where all the files containing trade disputes and their settlement are kept.'

'Good,' Belaru said exhaling a whiff of hot air from his nostrils. 'You have done very well. It is now the turn of the structural engineers to tell us the quality of the building of the trade foundation and the bomb launchers to tell us at what distance the bombs would be launched to have the desired impact and how many bombs are needed for the job.'

The structural engineers said the building was a concrete cast with re-enforcing iron bars. It was the strongest kind of building standing on a solid foundation.

The bomb launchers, having listened to the decipherers and structural engineers, were brief in their estimation of the range to launch the attack and the bombs required to do so. Five bombs were required and should be launched at a distance of three kilometers.

Chapter Eighteen

The Tendu-Purgers attack on the World Trade Foundation took place in the full gaze of the sun while employees of the foundation were at work. The timing was deliberate. It was informed by the war cry of the purgers:

Hit those who sustain the system!
Hit those who benefit from the system!
Bomb the system!
What the world needs is fairness, not charity.
Let's be fair to everyone.
And there will be no need for so-called charity.

For those who saw the attack, it was the most horrifying spectacle to watch as bomb after bomb landed on the World Trade Foundation with devastating effect. After the last bomb landed nothing was left of the World Trade Foundation, but ashes, dust and mangled iron rods.

Shrieks and screams of people caught in the attack could be heard by those sufficiently close to the building when the attack was going on. When the first bomb hit the building, some people inside the building jumped out through windows, most of them to their death. Shrieks and screams heard from the rubbles of the building were mostly of people on the ground floor who were buried in the ruins of the building. Before help could come, one of them was able to struggle out of the ruins of the building, his face a mask of blood and his entire body covered with dust and ash. He looked like a ghostly figure in a horror movie.

Palls of smoke billowed into the sky in dark balls and rivulets of soot and ruin. When a head count of the dead was taken, about five hundred people were confirmed dead. For hours, a pall of smoke hung over where the Foundation used to be as if it was the new Trade Foundation. The pall of smoke and ashes over the ruins of the Foundation looked like volcanic ash after a volcanic eruption.

Two men standing about three hundred meters from the building could not believe what they were seeing. Could this be the action of people made in the image of God or of the devil? How could this evil act proceed from the mind of a person having any bond with human beings?

'This is terrible,' said one of the men.

'It is indeed terrible,' said the other man.

'How can anyone with human blood and a human heart do a thing like this?' asked the first man. 'It is too chilling to contemplate and too shocking to see.'

'The heart of man is desperately wicked you know,' said the second man. 'It is from this wicked heart this horrendous specter proceeded.'

'The heart of man is also tender. It is on this tender heart the horrendous specter had fallen,' said the first man.

'You have also said something there,' said the second man.

'Why do people always want to invoke hell, to conjure hell as if it were rain to terrorize others?' the first man asked, rhetorically.

'I never thought I will see something like this in real life,' said the second man. 'When the first bomb dropped, I pinched myself to wake up, for I thought I was dreaming.'

'No doubt you are dreaming. This is a nightmare,' said the first man.

'But where is God? Why should he allow things like this to happen? Has he surrendered the world to the devil?' the second man asked, rhetorically.

'From what I am seeing, it seems so,' said the first man. 'We claim we are better than animals, but whenever we act, we embarrass animals,' he went on after a momentary pause. 'Imagine how animals will look at this action.'

'What are the grievances of the person who did this? Was there no one he could speak to for his grievances to be redressed? What sense of injustice moved him to this dastardly act?' said the second man.

'You said something there,' said the first man. 'There's rarely anyone these days to listen to another's grievances. Everyone is so much about himself without sparing care and love for others. This is the result.'

'We are heading to hell.'

'Are we? It looks like the devil and hell are already here.'

Help from rescue operations was long in coming. When it came, there was little to salvage from the wreckage of the bombs.

Chapter Nineteen

Tendu-Purgers attack on the World Trade Foundation provoked angry reactions around the world. The knee-jerk reaction of most developed nations was that it was another attack from an Islamic fundamentalist group. But no Islamic fundamentalist group claimed ownership of the attack. Instead, a secular terror organization that called itself Tendu-Purgers claimed to be responsible for the attack. It said it carried out the attack because of the exploitative, unjust and unfair economic relations between developed nations and developing nations. Unless world leaders redress the economic injustice being done to developing countries by developed nations, the world should say farewell to peace from this point on.

The world was stunned. This was preposterous, leaders of developed nations seethed. In a telephone conversation between the Saton President and Gebas Prime Minister, the Saton President livid with rage fumed, 'We won't negotiate with terrorists. No amount of blackmail will make us negotiate with terrorists.'

'This sounds good on phone and great on the screen, but in the real world out there, sometimes one has to negotiate with terrorists or they continue to feast on you,' said the Gebas Prime Minister.

'You are not suggesting we negotiate with terrorists?' asked the Saton President with a note of disbelief.

'I am not; neither do these terrorists seem to want to negotiate with us,' said the Gebas Prime Minister. 'Their demand that we do justice to developing nations does not sound like an invitation to us to negotiate with them. It sounds like an order for us to act.'

'And who are they to order us around?'

'They are terrorists who wear you out with guerilla warfare until nothing of you is left.'

'Fine, we are ready for them.'

'Are we? As for fine, I think we are not fine; we are sick.'

'Hello!'

'Hello!'

'Is it the Prime Minister of Gebas I am speaking with or one of the terrorists?'

'You are speaking with the Gebas Prime Minister alright. You see this secular terror organization unnerves me. It brings with it a historic claim for justice that makes me feel uneasy when I place it against the role played by my country and even by your country in shaping the current economic order.'

'Holy Mary.'

'This is the point. This secular terror organization does not understand holy Mary or holy Mohammed or holy Buddha. It is proving the corpse of the hunchback that would not enter the grave whichever way you turn it. There's no institution that can be used to appeal to it and no scripture to be cited for it or urged on it. Neither can it be blackmailed, for it seemed to be speaking for everyone, including us in the long term.'

'What I am hearing is like a terror attack on me.'

'Like I said before, this terror group is the corpse of the hunchback that would not enter the grave.'

'If it will not enter the grave, who goes into the grave?'

'Perhaps us.'

'Well, this grave was not dug for us.'

'Jokes apart, if it will not enter the grave, it means it can't be buried. So we have to live with it on the surface of the earth. The stench and the sight will not be pleasant.'

'What then do you suggest we do?' the Saton President asked trying unsuccessfully to keep exasperation out of his voice.

'Right now, honestly I don't know. I am a little confused.'

'You seem so.'

'Ahh....'

'Perhaps, we should call a world peace conference to discuss the matter.'

'Where they would bomb all of us out?'

'What!'

'They have said farewell to peace.'

'Very bad.'

'Yes, very bad. Besides, I don't think a peace conference would be helpful as far as this terror organization is concerned. They will rather you call a conference on world justice. I personally do not think much about conferences. They are mere talk shows and talk shops. They don't solve problems. What is needed to deal with this terror group is a workshop of action.'

'You seem to be saying something here.'

'We have been having workshops of action, but instead of having less terror, we are having more. Honestly, our so-called workshops of action are progressively looking like sowing terrorism. The terror harvest we are having seems to support what I am saying. Don't you think we should change tactics?'

'And do what? Negotiate with them?'

'No, not negotiate with them, but introduce some form of equity into our economic relations with developing nations.'

'That's worse than negotiating with them; that's surrendering to them. That will not happen. They are saying farewell to peace; farewell to peace then. We will hunt them down like the reptiles they are and kill them with bludgeon or rifle. We will smoke them out of their crevices and holes and club them to death.'

Chapter Twenty

In the Sekia Mountains, the Tendu-Purgers listened and watched world reaction to their attack of the World Trade Foundation. The reactions were not very different from what they expected. So they were neither disappointed nor surprised.

A week after the attack, Belaru was in Sekia Mountains talking with fellow purgers. They began talking on foreign investment.

'Foreign investment; how much do they put in? How much do they take out?' a purger asked.

'They are fishermen,' Belaru said. 'They take tiny baits to the river and return with a lot of fish. Sometimes they don't even take any bait to the river. It is in the river they get the bait. But they will still return home with a lot of fish. It seems to me more of foreign harvest than foreign investment.'

'It is so unfair,' said a purger.

'All this while they have been investing here, yet when you look, you don't see much. Are we baskets into which water is being poured?' said yet another purger.

'Well, you know they say we are basket cases,' said a purger in a derisive tone. 'So maybe we should blame ourselves if their investments are leaking out.'

'What nature gave us they are taking away,' lamented Belaru. 'Look, they have taken water by polluting the rivers and streams. No more clean rivers or streams you can get pure water from. The clean rivers and streams you can drink pure water from are now in sachets and bottles, and to drink this pure water you must pay; you lose money, they gain money; money leaves your pocket and enters their pocket; you are poorer, they are richer. After drinking the water in a sachet, you pay for its disposal or you find yourself in a nest of bottles or sachets. You pay for disposal, you lose money; they gain money; money leaves your pocket and enters their pocket; you are poorer, they are richer. They are eating us out of house and home.'

'It irks hearing all these and knowing them to be true,' a purger seethed.

'What we used to get freely we now pay for. We are always taking money out of our pockets without taking any inside,' Belaru continued. 'Worms and rats are eating us out of house and home.'

'It rankles to think of all these,' said a purger.

'Instead of telling developing nations or at least allowing them to save and develop, they cajole and arm-twist them into borrowing money from them to develop,' Belaru continued sounding a shade bitter. 'Of course, they do this so that their money does not lie idle. It should go out and bring more money through usury. Debt-funded development has turned poor, developing nations into debt-junkies that cannot survive without fixes. These fixes instead of fixing developing nations unfix them.'

'It needless knowing all these,' raged a purger.

'They don't respect the right of a country not to develop,' Belaru went on. 'Even if you say you don't want to develop, they will say you must; why? Because in your so-called development is their gain. To develop, you have to borrow money from their banks; you have to hire the services of their experts; you have to buy their goods. This is profit to them if it isn't to you. We are being eaten out of house and home.'

'It festers knowing all these,' mourned a purger.

'It is not today this cheating, stealing and deception started,' Belaru resumed after a moment of silence. 'Things have always been like this throughout history. About two hundred years ago, Chelida refused to accept loans from Gebas and also refused to sign up to free trade, it was invaded by the so-called Chekas Alliance of Texki, Linga and Hendel who were mere Gebas puppets. Also about two hundred years ago, when Fagula resisted the attempt by Gebas to smuggle wenga – a dangerous narcotic drug into Fagula to alter its unfavorable balance of trade with Fagula, Fagula was invaded.'

'That was so unfair.'

'Just imagine the iniquity, the immorality, the lack of conscience of declaring war on a country because the invaded country refused to allow a dangerous narcotic drug to be smuggled into it.'

'It is horrible merely thinking about it.'

'It sure is.'

'But today there are provisions in free trade agreements a nation can take advantage of to protect itself from the debilitating effect of free trade.'

'There are. Unfortunately, loan conditionalities on free trade makes it impossible for them to take advantage of these provisions.'

'Really sad.'

'Really sad, indeed.

'Talking about provisions in free trade agreements we may take advantage of has set me thinking in a terrible direction,' said a purger with the face of a hangman.

'What terrible direction are you thinking?' asked another purger.

'If some people were enslaved because they were supposed to be monkeys and chimps, can't they in turn enslave the real monkeys and chimps out there in the jungle?' said the purger with the face of a hangman.

'They can; unfortunately, however, slavery has ran out of fashion,' Belaru said. 'The steam engine made slavery unnecessary and in fact wasteful. Besides, doing what you propose will be misplaced aggression. People that were enslaved should target those who messed them up, not innocent chimps and monks out there.'

'We have a historic duty to deal with a historic injustice once and for all times,' said a purger with touching anger.

'Yes, we do,' Belaru enthused. 'But there's Akkub,' he murmured to himself. 'All developed nations cannot be bad if Okla a developed nation can have a good man like Akkub.'

'We can't hear what you are saying?

'No, no, no, I was only talking to my troubled mind,' Belaru said, feigning cheer.

Chapter Twenty-One

After the telephone conversation between the Saton President and the Gebas Prime Minister, Saton activated its diplomatic network across the globe particularly in developed nations. Saton would not stand by and watch a bunch of misguided elements risk fortunes it had gone to great lengths to secure over the centuries.

'Terrorism is a global scourge that requires international cooperation to contain, if not flush out,' the Saton President said to the Oklan Prime Minister who was in Netalu to register the support of his country for Saton's declaration of war against global terrorism.

'Okla cannot agree with you more,' said the Oklan Prime Minister. 'We are victims of terrorism and therefore know what it is.'

'We will take them out however long it takes us to do so. They can't expose us this way and live to laugh at us,' the Saton President vowed.

'Yes, we have to take them out before they take us out; no, before they take us in,' said the Oklan Prime Minister. 'We stand shoulder to shoulder with you on this.'

'Can we look at what they are demanding?' asked the Melili Prime Minister who was also in Netalu with the Saton President and the Oklan Prime Minister.

'No, no, no,' shrieked the Saton President. 'What they are demanding is that we place our heads on the slaughter slab. No one hearkens to that kind of demand.'

'Okla is also with you there,' said the Oklan Prime Minister.

'There's a sense in which their insisting we should be fair to developing countries in our economic relationship is more dangerous than religious fundamentalism,' said the Saton President. 'If we accede to this, how do we continue to be rich and powerful?'

'Now, I can see the danger,' said the Melili Prime Minister. 'In future, I foresee them asking for reparation for past gains we made in our unfair economic relationship with the developing nations. You can imagine how much we would have to vomit out. You can imagine our ruination.'

'I wonder why Gebas is not seeing the matter the way we are?' said the Oklan Prime Minister.

'It is not Gebas that is not seeing the matter our way,' said the Saton President. 'It is the Gebas Prime Minister. Gebas citizens do not share his sentiments of justice. Anyway, very soon he would pay a heavy political price for toeing the line of the terrorists. Elections are around the corner in Gebas.'

'How do we nail the Tendu-Purgers?' asked the Melili Prime Minister.

'By activating our intelligence networks the way we have activated our diplomatic networks,' said the Saton President. 'With proper intelligence gathering, we will know who they are, where they are and who is funding them. Already we know their leader is called Belaru and they are in Blufor only we don't know which region of that vast country.'

'Intelligence is an awesome thing,' said the Melili Prime Minister. 'Whoever has intelligence on a secret or a clandestine activity, in some way, is God over the matter.'

'That's true, said the Oklan Prime Minister. 'After all, God is God because he is all-knowing. Particularly with the surge in global terrorism, we have to take the science of intelligence to the next level. We should go beyond gathering intelligence on the location and moves of terrorists to knowing what they are thinking.'

'Shh …,' the Melili Prime Minister muttered, making a hushing sign at the Oklan Prime Minister. 'We are thinking and talking like the devil or at least his demons. If God hears what we are saying, he will side with the terrorists against us.'

'I am not sure if he has not already done so,' murmured the Oklan Prime Minister. 'Well, if he sides with them, someone who is never on the same side with him will side with us.'

'Sacrilege, taboo, abomination,' the Melili Prime Minister murmured, cringing his body in seeming revulsion.

'Talking about thinking and talking like God, have we ever thought and acted like God?' snickered the Saton President. 'By the way, are the terrorists themselves thinking and acting like God? This is an entirely devil's affair. We are better off tangling with the guy with horns and a tail than the pious one.'

'How do we evolve the type of intelligence you are recommending?' the Melili Prime Minister asked the Oklan Prime Minister.

'I don't know. But I know with science and technology, everything is possible. If we will ever be God, it will only be through science and technology.'

'Well, we shall see about that,' said the Melili Prime Minister. 'But before getting to that promised land, we must do our best to survive by current devices of intelligence gathering. Putting such devices to effective use, we can abort all clandestine and nefarious activities of the terrorists.'

'That's true,' said the Saton President. 'Let's stick together, let's hold hands on this matter and I am sure we will flush them out before they embarrass us further.'

'Flush them out before they flush us out! This should be our own war cry,' said the Melili Prime Minister.

'Yes, let's stick together, let's hold hands on this matter,' the Oklan Prime Minister, with a grim expression on his face, rehashed what the Saton President had said. 'Let's stick together, perhaps not only with ourselves, but with the guy with the tail and horns.'

'You are on your own there,' said the Melili Prime Minister. Addressing the Saton President, he said, 'we are with you comrade where you are.'

After this discussion, the Melili and Oklan Prime Ministers returned to their countries and read the riot act to their intelligence departments.

Chapter Twenty-Two

Ten years after the World Trade Foundation attack, Belaru and his Tendu-Purgers launched wildcat attacks on synagogues, churches, mosques, courts and universities in different countries of the world. As with the World Trade Foundation attacks, their war cry remained:

Hit those who sustain the system!
Hit those who benefit from the system!
Bomb the system!
What the world needs is fairness, not charity.
Let's be fair to everyone.
And there will be no need for so-called charity.

The carpet bombing on almost all continents of the world was to tell the world the Tendu-Purgers were in every country and could strike anywhere and anytime. This was also to tell the world the institutions they were after. The attacks took everyone, particularly world leaders, by surprise. After ten years of no one hearing anything about the Tendu-Purgers, the world was gradually lulled into believing the group had fizzled out. It was, therefore, a rude shock for most world leaders particularly in the developed countries to be reminded of the existence of the purgers in this emphatic manner.

It was part of the strategy of Tendu-Purgers to now and then go underground and off the radar of security agents that were out to rout and emasculate them. Also going underground gave them time to plan for future attacks. When they went underground after the World Trade Foundation attack, they used the opportunity to open new Tendu-Purgers cells and to carefully select their next targets of attack, their location and the timing of the attacks. In Saton, they picked a pharmaceutical company in Besie; In Desia, they picked a national bank in Kolow; in Rotta they picked a law firm in Melili and an investment corporation in Wemak; in Tekinna, they picked a mosque in Baram and a synagogue in Okla; in Ponto, they picked a university in Tenkan.

All these institutions were hit at about the same time with flash-striker bombs delivered by sacko launchers. Before the attacks, Belaru again spoke to the purgers on the historic injustice done to developing nations by developed countries and the need for historic vengeance.

'Babua rice required neither pesticides nor fertilizer,' he said to the purgers. 'The seeds of this rice could also be stored for use the following year. Saton introduced tratos rice that requires pesticides, fertilizer and could not be stored for planting another year. Babua farmers were brainwashed and arm-twisted to abandon Babua rice for tratos rice which is said to be high-yielding than Babua rice. Now, Babua farmers have to buy pesticides, fertilizer and rice seedlings every year from Saton. Babua is poorer; Saton is richer.'

'God will punish them.'

'No, we will punish them,' Belaru said with vigor. 'Some years ago, the high-yielding tratos rice introduced into Babua could not withstand pests' attacks despite the pesticides used to fumigate the pests. There was massive crop failure and Babua rice farmers ravaged by famine and debts committed suicide by drinking the pesticides. If the pesticides could not kill the pests, they should kill them and end their sorrow.'

'So sad.'

'Yes, so sad. We are the refuse dump for their toxic wastes. International law exists allowing them to take their hazardous industrial wastes to us for disposal. They eat the corn and throw the cob at us.'

'God, where are you?'

'I don't know; but I know we will attack the institutions they use to impoverish and mess us up. We will attack legal institutions, synagogues, churches, mosques, investment houses, banks and educational institutions for their complicity in crime.'

After this declaration of intent, the marked institutions were attacked in a shocking carpet bombing the world had never known or thought possible. While the dusts of the attacks were yet to settle, Belaru was speaking to Tendu-Purgers in a Tendu cell in a forest in Dirasa:

'We hit law … '

'Because law is politics of oppression.'

'We hit the synagogues and the mosques ...'

'Because these religious institutions are politics of domination and do not denounce the demonic cheating of poor nations by rich nations.'

'We hit investment houses ...'

'Because they are fishermen taking far in excess of what they put in.'

'We hit banks ...'

'Because of their usurious leading.

'We are the hand and sword of justice ...'

'Forever raised against cheating, exploitation and oppression.'

'If God is on the side of the strongest army ...'

'We are the devil that is on the side of the weakest army.'

Two days after reciting these reasons among themselves, the Tendu-Purgers caused the reasons to be published in the World Times magazine.

Chapter Twenty-Three

It was difficult to tell whether the world was more shaken by the attacks or the reasons for them advanced by the purgers. Whichever was the case, world leaders were rattled by the purgers. What they thought had fizzled out was merely hibernating and incubating. In terms of scale and popular appeal, the attacks were unprecedented.

At home, the wife of the Saton President advised her husband to consider the demands of the terrorist so that the world can know peace once more.

'Has the world ever known peace?' the President asked in a sardonic tone.

'What are you saying?' the wife asked somewhat aghast.

'The world in case you are a stranger in it has never known peace,' said the President. 'Even the grand old book says that from the very beginning the kingdom of God suffereth violence and only the violent can take it by force.'

'The Kingdom of God is not the kingdom of men.'

'That makes it worse,' quipped the President. 'If the kingdom of God suffers violence, that of men should suffer upheavals of cataclysmic proportion.'

'Just spare time and consider what the terrorists are saying.'

'While I spare time to consider what they are saying, they are sparing no time and opportunity to annihilate me. You have heard their war cry: *Hit those who sustain the system*! *Hit those who benefit from the system*! *Bomb the system*! I sustain the system; I benefit from the system, and in a sense, I am the system. So, there's no escape hatch for me. *Let's be fair to everyone* as if everyone is someone! *Spare time and consider what they are saying,* when they are sparing death for me? My dear, you don't know who these cranks are!'

Even without them saying it, I have always felt the world needs more justice than I see around. Spare a thought for justice my ego.'

'My dear you have a good heart, the heart of a deer. But these guys are hyenas with the hearts of wolves. While the deer is interceding for the hyena, the hyena most certainly is howling for the deer's meat.'

'Perhaps you are right. But we can't all be hyenas. The growling and howling will be too much for the world. I think some of us need to be deer to recover hyenas. Spare consideration for justice, my ego.'

'My dear, we can't afford the justice they are demanding. We will be out of business if we can. We will not be rich if we can. At whatever cost, we must sustain the current order.'

'What you are saying sounds sick to me.'

'Well, we are in a sick world. The crackbrains that blew up our pharmaceutical company did not tell me they are well. They told me they are sick and are not interested in a cure. Why should I be the one that is well or interested in a cure?'

'What!'

'Yes, my dear; not only did they tell me they are sick and need no cure, they told me they are in fact against all the cures in the world – hence their attack on a pharmaceutical company.

Inspite of herself, the President's wife could not suppress a chuckle.

'My dear, if there's God, he never meant the world to be fair and just. At least that's what I see. It is all about survival of the fittest and everyone to himself. If God has no agenda of justice, why should Saton? Saton cannot be more Godly than God.'

'I can't bear hearing any more of these,' said the wife, walking hurriedly away.

Sitting alone in his office later, the Saton President was thinking of the attacks. What the attacks showed was that Saton's intelligence network was not working well. Security intelligence reports he got before the attacks had nothing either on the Tendu-Purgers or their impending attacks. This showed total failure of intelligence gathering and someone must pay for it. He called his chief intelligence officer to his office to demand explanation.

'Honestly sir, I don't know how they were able to be completely off our radar the way they were,' said the intelligence chief.

'I hope they were not off your radar because you had no radar.'

'No sir, we had radar.'

'You had some intelligence on these guys, but thought they presented less danger to us?' the President asked, his eyes probing the intelligence chief.

'No sir. By no means will we fall into such security inertia. In our work, every security risk must continuously be taken seriously,' said the intelligence chief.

'This sounds good if your failure is embarrassing,' said the President. 'In the dangerous world we live in today, intelligence often makes the difference between life and death. If you had any doubt before, the Tendu-Purgers' recent wildcat attacks must have removed such doubt.'

'We are sorry sir.'

'How will your penitence or apology help those that were killed; those whose property were destroyed?' asked the President. 'How will it help the orphans of those that were killed or their widows?'

'We are sorry.'

'Can you imagine the insult?'

'Yes sir.'

'Oh, so you can imagine the insult and yet allowed it to happen?'

'I don't mean it that way, sir.'

'Can you imagine the embarrassment?'

'No sir.'

'Oh, so because you could not imagine the embarrassment you allowed it to happen.'

'Sorry, I don't mean it that way sir.'

'We are living in a world full of crackbrains who would not give a hoot if the whole world is blown off as long as that will advance their cranky ideas and fantasy. In such a world, an intelligence officer has to wear his thinking cap all the time and be one jump ahead of the cranks all the time. You seemed not to be wearing your thinking cap always and that's why a bunch of lunatics can pass this type of shit under our nose. The world is a place of responsibilities. You have yours. I have mine. If you omit to discharge your responsibilities and something goes wrong, you pay a price. The same goes for me. Because you failed to perform your responsibilitities, we have been shown to be an easy target. This is an insult. For allowing this insult to be spat on Saton, I hereby relieve you of your job as chief intelligence officer. In doing so, I am only discharging the responsibility I owe the Saton people as President. You may go.'

'Please sir.'

'I am out of the humor of mercy.'

Chapter Twenty-Four

After the carpet bombings in all parts of the world, Belaru returned to Sekia Mountains, the headquarters of the war against injustice. There was a marked improvement in his cheer. It seemed the wildcat attacks had tickled his funny bone. He was a student of history. He could not remember reading of any time attacks of a widespread nature like the ones the Tendu-Purgers just carried out ever happened. Not only were the attacks phenomenally widespread, they were monstrously successful. The attacks were the kind of global message he wanted to send and he had sent it. The world and the powers that be in it whether they liked it or not would not only have to reckon with them but with their message as well.

In the Sekia Mountains, Tendu-Purgers were in an ecstatic mood. It was from the Sekia Mountains the crusade against injustice began. Whatever it eventually becomes, the Sekia Mountains had a pride of place in that thing. When the crusade started in the Sekia Mountains, some of them never gave it the chance of success it was now having. Now they were the focus of world attention and the envy of other terrorist organizations. There was hardly any world news or global debate on terrorism that they didn't get mentioned. It now looked like so-called world powers feared them than they feared the devil.

Belaru was given a rousing reception on his return. The insurgency was his vision and the able way it had been handled was also largely a function of his management.

'Razanu was a fifty percent pastoral and a fifty percent agricultural country,' Belaru said amidst the euphoria of his reception. 'Razanu was brainwashed and railroaded to take an IMF loan. When it could neither repay the principal nor service the interests, it was manipulated to abandon farming in favor of pastoralism to be able to at least service the loan. Razanu did as it was directed. The result was that too many cattle laid the country bare by eating all its vegetation. Without vegetation, the water cycle of Razanu was disrupted. The atmosphere could no longer get from plants the water that used to evaporate from them into it. Having less water in it, the atmosphere produced less rain. Razanu was caught in cycles of droughts that led to famine. When rain managed to fall, runoffs carried away arable soil from Razanu to the sea.'

'Really sad,' mourned the Tendu-Purgers.

'Today, there are certain parts of Gogan that have not known rain for five years,' Belaru continued. 'The reason is that aerosol, a pollutant from industrial production in developed countries, is migrating to Gogan to suppress clouds formation thereby preventing rain from falling. They are eating and farting, but we are the ones suffering the smell.'

'How will this not get us raving mad?' fumed a purger.

'Yes, why shouldn't it?' said Belaru. 'That's why we are raving and they will not like how long and loud we will rave,' he continued after a momentary pause. 'From a baby that could not sit, we now have one that can sit, crawl, walk, run and even jump. That's how well we are growing.'

'It is so thrilling to see,' said a purger.

'So, pleasing to be part of,' said another purger.

'Where we are is not our destiny …,' said Belaru.

'We will use violence to grow into our destiny,' his fellow purgers finished off for him.

'The world is a prostitute …'

'She sleeps with whoever can pay.'

'They can pay, and pay in wads of greenbacks…'

'So the world has since been in their inns.'

'They pay the world with wads of money …'

'Stolen from us.'

'We have risen from the poverty they exported to us …'

'And are at the gates of their inns calling on the prostitute to come to us, for we too can pay, and pay in blood.'

'The world is now flowering with retribution …'

'But bees are not about the flowers for nectar and pollen to make honey of peace.'

'They may not give us what we want – justice …'

'We will not fail to give them what they want – war.'

'If they are miserly …'

'We are generous especially if our generosity will lead to their death.'

'Peace is the happy child of justice…'

'War is the unhappy child of injustice that developed nations impregnated the world with. The child has been delivered and is now looking for the father to avenge his misery.'

'If they have forgotten what justice is …'

'We will not forget what nemesis and retribution are.'

'We will rather die in the last ditch …'

'Than surrender.'

'But there's Akkub,' Belaru mourned softly. 'All developed nations cannot be bad if Okla a developed nation can have a good man like Akkub.'

www.ingramcontent.com/pod-product-compliance
Lightning Source LLC
Chambersburg PA
CBHW051458130726
47987CB00005B/2376